Dear Reader:

LOVESWEPT celebrates heroes, those irresistible men who sweep us off our feet, who tantalize us with whispered endearments, and who challenge us with their teasing humor and hidden vulnerability. Whether they're sexy roughnecks or dashing sophisticates, dark and dangerous or blond and brash, these men are heartthrobs, the kind no woman can get enough of. And now, just in time for Valentine's Day, all six books in this month's line-up have truly special covers that feature only these gorgeous heartthrobs. HEARTTHROBS—heroes who'll leave you spellbound as only real men can, in six fabulous new romances by only the best in the genre.

### Don't miss any of our HEARTTHROBS this month

There's no better way to celebrate the most romantic day of the year than to cuddle up with all six LOVESWEPT HEARTTHROBS!

With best wishes,

*Nita Taublib*

Nita Taublib
Associate Publisher/LOVESWEPT

## WHAT ARE *LOVESWEPT* ROMANCES?

They are stories of true romance and touching emotion. We believe those two very important ingredients are constants in our highly sensual and very believable stories in the *LOVESWEPT* line. Our goal is to give you, the reader, stories of consistently high quality that may sometimes make you laugh, sometimes make you cry, but are always fresh and creative and contain many delightful surprises within their pages.

Most romance fans read an enormous number of books. Those they truly love, they keep. Others may be traded with friends and soon forgotten. We hope that each *LOVESWEPT* romance will be a treasure—a "keeper." We will always try to publish

*LOVE STORIES YOU'LL NEVER FORGET*
*BY AUTHORS YOU'LL ALWAYS REMEMBER*

The Editors

## Jan Hudson
### Call Me Sin

**BANTAM BOOKS**
NEW YORK · TORONTO · LONDON · SYDNEY · AUCKLAND

CALL ME SIN

*A Bantam Book / March 1992*

*If you would be interested in receiving protective vinyl
covers for your Loveswept books, please write to this address
for information:*

> Loveswept
> Bantam Books
> P.O. Box 985
> Hicksville, NY 11802

ISBN 0-553-44089-6

*Published simultaneously in the United States and Canada*

PRINTED IN THE UNITED STATES OF AMERICA

OPM      0 9 8 7 6 5 4 3 2 1

*For all the fine folks in Beaumont,
especially the dedicated members of the GTWG.
And thanks again to Sergeant Don Morris,
Company A, Texas Rangers, and the cooperative
staff of Company A Headquarters.*

*Thanks to Rose
for the Great Escape*

# One

Susan Sinclair heard an ominous *thunk* behind her.

The bottom dropped out of her stomach, and a terrible feeling of dread washed over her, draining blood from her face and puddling it in the general area of her kneecaps.

*Oh, please, Lord, no.*

Scurrying back to the door, coffee sloshing over the rim of her Sherlock Holmes mug, she jiggled the unyielding knob. The worst scenario had come to pass.

She was locked out of her town house.

Tugging at the pink undershirt that barely skimmed the tops of her French-cut panties, she surveyed the oak-lined street. All quiet. The only thing stirring was Mrs. Jenkins's Siamese cat three doors down. And one corner of the *Beaumont Enterprise* flapped in the fall breeze, taunting her from the sidewalk four feet away. She glared at the paper that had caused her predicament and poked mental pins into an image of the paper boy.

She raked a hand through her sleep-tangled hair and leaned her forehead against the door. How could she have done something so stupid? Something that only happened in TV sitcoms? What had possessed her to make a dash for the paper without putting on a robe? She *never* did such rash things. But then, the delivery boy always put the *Enterprise* just outside her door.

What was she going to do?

Illogically, she tugged and twisted and rattled the door as if some miracle would save her from the mess she was in. The blue door held firm.

Behind her she heard the roar of a truck coming up the street, and she scrambled for a camellia bush at the edge of her small porch. Since it had been planted only a few months before, the camellia didn't provide much cover. The plant was only waist high, and its spindly limbs were sparsely leafed, but some cover was better than nothing. She crouched behind it and prayed that the truck would pass on by.

Her pulse quickened as a big, candy-apple-red pickup festooned with chrome fog lamps and a roll bar pulled to a stop at the curb. For a moment she forgot her dilemma as she peered over the top of the bush and, mesmerized, watched a huge, swarthy man climb out.

A red bandanna circled his forehead and was tied at the back of a shock of hair that was thick, wavy, and midnight black. Well-worn jeans with a rip in the knee hung low on his lean hips, and their frayed bottoms brushed a pair of scuffed roper boots.

His faded gray T-shirt stretched across yard-wide shoulders and a broad, muscled chest. The jagged armholes of the garment looked as if he'd ripped them out with his teeth, and the thing must have shrunk in the dryer because its hem stopped an inch shy of his belly button.

He was fantasy in human form, like something she'd only seen in movies. She could tell at a glance that he was a real man, one who could handle anything. Something about him brought to mind the strength and stealth of a predator.

He reached into the bed of the truck and his biceps bulged as he slung a duffel bag over one shoulder and hoisted a big backpack onto the other. He walked straight toward her and, as she looked into eyes as black as an eagle's talons, her knees sagged. His cheekbones were broad and high like an Indian warrior's. She could imagine him, a hundred years ago, with feathers in his hair and a quiver of arrows on his back, clad only in a leather breechclout. A ripple skittered up her spine.

"Good morning," he said to her in a rumbling bass.

Mortified that she'd been caught in such an awful predicament, she closed her eyes and prayed fervently that the earth would open up and swallow her.

The earth didn't move.

Since her guardian angel seemed to be on sabbatical, there was nothing for her to do but cope on her own. *Act nonchalant*, she told herself. Still trying to hide as much as possible behind the bush, she straightened, gathered the spindly branches around her like a hula skirt, and took a sip from the mug she clutched in her hand.

"Good morning," she returned in a squeak that she barely recognized as her own voice.

"You live here?" His gaze flicked over her, and he smiled. And, oh, what a smile. It crinkled his eyes, cut deep brackets down his cheeks, and showed a mouth full of the straightest, whitest teeth she'd ever seen. The man was drop-dead handsome—if you went for the rough, rugged type. And she was quickly beginning to think she did.

Awestruck, she tightened her fingers around the mug and clutched the branches tighter around her middle. For some reason, she wanted to impress him, act the *femme fatale*, say something clever, but her brain and her body wouldn't cooperate. Also, talking with a Greek god was difficult when one was dressed in a camellia bush. "Yes. Here."

"Then it looks like we're going to be neighbors."

"Neighbors?"

"I'm Ross Berringer." He cocked his head toward the town house next door. "I'm leasing that place."

"That place?" Her eyes were fascinated by his belly button. Holding the load on his shoulder had hiked his skimpy shirt up even farther. His abdomen was corded like a washboard. Her knees twitched and she clutched the mug even tighter.

"Yep. And you're . . . ?"

She glanced up and was captivated by his magnificent eyes. She ached to do a swan dive into their black depths and loll in the provocative promises they made. Tantalizing images of steamy nights and lustful transgressions filled her mind.

"You're . . . ?" he prompted in his wonderful deep voice.

"Susan Sinclair." In her throatiest Bacall imitation she added, "But call me Sin."

"Sin?" Amusement tinged his question.

Reality flooded back into the moment and brought a flush to her face. What had ever possessed her to say such a thing? She fought the embarrassment and brazened it out. "Sure. Sin . . . Sinclair, a logical nickname." She didn't add that nobody had ever called her Sin.

"I'm happy to meet my new neighbor." His gaze passed over her in blatant perusal, and his engaging grin was one of roguish merriment. "Can I come over later to borrow a cup of sugar . . . Sin?"

She shifted nervously, unable to think of a snappy rejoinder. How had she gotten herself in this mess? Now he probably thought she was the neighborhood bimbo. "Uh, sure."

"The manager of the complex is supposed to meet me here with the key," Ross said. "You haven't seen her, have you?"

Relief flooded her. "The manager? Oh, thank heavens!"

He looked puzzled.

"I'm locked out. I only wanted to get the newspaper," she explained, "but a gust of wind must have slammed the door. I was afraid I'd have to break a window to get in."

He grinned. "Aw shucks, you mean you don't always run around in your skivvies?"

She wanted to die of humiliation, but she raised her chin and gave him her most quelling look, the one she'd learned in Introduction to Library Science to shush noisy patrons. "Hardly. How indelicate of you to mention it."

He wiped the grin from his face, but his eyes still danced with mischief. "Yes, ma'am."

She was saved from further indignity when the manager's little blue car screeched to a stop at the curb. After a quick explanation of the situation, the manager unlocked Susan's door with her master key.

"Please turn your head," Susan said to the big man, who remained standing in her front yard. Hoping that he'd complied with her request, Susan scampered inside.

When the door closed behind her, she leaned back against it. The first man she'd met in ages who made her heart go pitty-pat, and she'd had to meet him in such an appalling situation! Something shriveled inside her. How could she ever face him again?

There was a knock at the door.

She opened it a crack and peered out.

Ross Berringer stood there smiling. "You forgot your newspaper." He handed it to her. "And Susan," he said before she could close the door, "you don't have to be embarrassed. I turned my head."

Susan arranged a new display in the window of her book store, then went outside to check the effect. She was trying to keep busy, trying to wipe the awkward encounter with her new neighbor from her mind, but it played over and over in her head.

"Hi, Susan," a feminine voice called. "You're in early this morning."

She started and turned to find her friend Linda Brewer, who owned the beauty salon two doors down from her bookstore, The Great Escape. "Oh, hi, Linda. I didn't hear you drive up. Did you and Don have a nice vacation?"

"If you can call two weeks with in-laws who think their baby boy married beneath him nice, I suppose so." The short, dark-haired woman wrinkled her pug nose. "The fall foliage in New England was pretty, but, let me tell you, I was glad to get back to good old Beaumont, Texas. Anything new and *exciting* happen around here while I was gone?" She raised her eyebrows and gave a teasing smile.

Splaying her hand across the bodice of her blue shirtwaist dress, Susan replied dramatically, "You mean something exciting like UPS delivering the wrong package to Salvador's Gun Shop or Hebert's Restaurant running out of crawfish for last week's Tuesday special?"

"No. I mean like Tom Cruise moving in next door or your winning the lottery."

"I didn't enter the lottery, and I can't imagine Tom Cruise leaving Hollywood. But I am getting a new neighbor."

Linda's eyes widened. "Male?"

Tucking an errant wisp into her neat chignon, Susan lifted her chin. "*Very.*"

"Sounds interesting. Tell me more."

"There's nothing to tell."

A white Buick pulled into a parking space in front of Rave Wave and tooted its horn. Linda grimaced. "Oh piddle, there's Mrs. Becker for her perm. I have to run, but I want to hear all the details later. Is he gorgeous?"

"Is who gorgeous? Tom Cruise? Oh, there's no question that Tom has a dynamite smile, but he's a little too short for my taste. And young. I think he's definitely too young for me. However—"

"*Not* Tom Cruise. I'm talking about the new neighbor you're trying to avoid discussing." Linda planted her fists on her hips. "Don't give me that innocent look, Susan Sinclair. I'm not fooled for a minute with that prim and proper librarian exterior. I'm your best friend, remember?"

After Linda hurried away, Susan studied her tall reflection in the large window where her dim image mingled with rows and rows of paperback books inside her shop. Prim and proper librarian?

She turned to the right and to the left, her perusal taking in everything from her sensible canvas espadrilles to the full-skirted dress with its Peter Pan collar. She stuck her face close to the window. Simple gold studs. Hair slicked into a neat coil. Minimal makeup. She did look like a librarian—which was not surprising. Until a year ago, she *had* been a librarian. And the university where she'd worked frowned on the professional staff wearing miniskirts and spike hairdos. Habit and the contents of her closet dictated her appearance. She shrugged and was about to go back inside when she heard a truck pull up behind her. In the window she saw the reflection of a familiar candy-apple-red pickup.

Her first impulse was to bolt, but, as if pulled

by a magnet, she turned and watched Ross Berringer step down from the cab. He still wore the same garb, and it was still as sexy as it had been earlier.

"Hello, again," he said. "The manager of the complex told me you had a bookstore here."

"Uh, yes. Do you need a book?" *Clever repartee, Susan. Really clever.*

He reached into the truck for a small bag and, holding the strap with two fingers, slung it over his shoulder. His short-cropped T-shirt rode up, and his belly button seemed to wink at her. He smiled. "Maybe later. Right now I need a gym."

"A gym?"

He gestured toward the fitness center cater-cornered from The Great Escape. "You know, for body building."

"You certainly have the body for it."

His belly shook as he laughed. She felt a hot flush creep up her throat, and she quickly averted her enthralled eyes from his navel. Had she really said that? She couldn't believe she'd said that. Something about this king-size specimen of manhood made her go a little crazy.

"Uh, uh, excuse me," she mumbled. "I think I hear my phone."

His muscles rippled as he shifted the bag on his shoulder. "Catch you later, neighbor."

"Later." She fled into the sanctity of The Great Escape and the familiar smell of aging paper.

Ignoring the display she'd been working on, she retreated into the mystery alcove and leaned back against the shelves. She popped open the top buttons of her dress and fanned her hot cheeks with a Sue Grafton novel.

Why had she acted so absolutely gauche? The

man outside was the living embodiment of every woman's dreams. She'd secretly fantasized about meeting someone like Ross, but had she matched his smoldering gaze with a scorching one of her own? No. Had she intrigued him with a mysterious smile or scintillating conversation? Oh, no. She'd behaved like a . . . a scared virgin. Which she wasn't. At least not the virgin part.

For five years she'd been married to Thomas Rowe, an archeology professor she'd met in the stacks soon after she began working as a librarian at Tulane University. Thomas was a truly nice man, but he was no Indiana Jones. No hidden fires burned in his breast, and he was about as exciting as cold grits. The only thing they had in common was their love of books. Gradually, their marriage had expired from boredom—hers more than his—and the last rites had been pronounced eighteen months before.

The hunk in the short T-shirt might be a lot of things, but she doubted that he would ever be boring. He certainly wasn't marriage material—and she wasn't in the market—but she'd bet he could make life exciting.

Still irritated with her bumbling interlude with the man, Susan muttered self rebukes and shoved the paperback back in the shelf. Before her castigations became too disheartening, the bell on the front door interrupted. She squared her shoulders and left her retreat.

"Good morning, Joe," she said to one of her regular customers. "I have in a new batch of science fiction that you'll want to see."

He nodded and strode to his usual area of

interest. Joe wasn't a talkative individual, but every week the ruddy-faced man came in for a book.

In the year since she'd moved back to Texas and bought The Great Escape, she'd developed a strong and loyal clientele of really nice people. She'd been ready for a change in her dull life, and when her grandmother had offered to finance her purchase of the bookstore, Susan had jumped at the chance. She wanted to live closer to her grandmother, and she'd always had fond memories of Beaumont. But her life, except in her fantasies, was still as boring and ordinary as ever. Maybe that's why she loved books so much—she could vicariously experience glamour, mystery, and excitement.

She sighed and, while Joe browsed, finished the window display and straightened the front counter.

A few other customers came and went before she had an opportunity to pick up the mystery novel she was dying to finish. Soon, she lost herself in the story.

A big hand passed over her face.

"Anybody home?" a deep voice said.

Jolted back into reality, Susan blinked. Ross Berringer, his hair a damp mass of black curls, stood across the counter from her, waving his hand across her face and grinning.

Her absorption with the story fled, and a flush crept over her face. "Sorry, I was engrossed in a murder. Have you finished your workout?"

"All done. Thought I'd grab a bite to eat before I go back to wait for the delivery people. Want to have lunch with me? I hear Hebert's on the corner is pretty good."

"If you like Cajun food, it's very good. But I can't leave the store."

A customer came in and Susan excused herself to help the woman find a special diet volume. When she returned, Ross was leaning against the counter and flipping through the pages of the latest Brax Knight novel she'd been reading.

"This looks pretty good," he said.

"I can recommend it."

"*You* read this kind of stuff?"

"Of course. Don't you approve?"

He chuckled. "Sure I approve. *I* read it. You just surprised me."

His surprise rankled. He probably thought she spent her spare time reading poetry and crocheting doilies. "I'm an avid mystery fan."

"Me too." Ross plucked a new copy of the novel from the rack beside the counter and thumbed the pages. "Boy, I wish I could write like this guy."

Susan sighed. "Doesn't everybody? Brax Knight is the best hero since Travis McGee. People are clamoring for more."

He laid his forearm across the counter and leaned closer. "Have you ever tried writing?" His voice gentled and his rugged face assumed a warmth and openness that encouraged confidences.

She had the strangest urge to throw herself into his arms and pour out her life story. Wistfully, she gazed off into space. "I once had visions of becoming the next John D. MacDonald or Evelyn Anthony."

"And?"

A twinge of self-consciousness prodded laughter from her. "And I have to be content with selling other people's books. I have no talent as a writer. Do you read much?"

"Quite a bit. You'll probably be seeing a lot of me, neighbor." He gave her a teasing wink and smiled.

Her toes curled in her espadrilles.

After he paid for the book and left, she was too busy with customers to think much about Ross. When Nadine Gex, the woman who worked part time for her, arrived, Susan gobbled a tuna fish sandwich for lunch, then restocked the shelves.

At five, Susan left Nadine to run the store until the six o'clock closing time and went home. The street was quiet and the candy-apple pickup was missing from the curb. On her way inside, she decided that her front windows looked dirty, and now was a perfect time to tackle them. They really needed cleaning she assured herself; she wasn't just doing it in hopes of catching another glimpse of Ross Berringer.

Half an hour later, the interior glass on her two front windows was spotless, and she'd almost finished with the outside. The red pickup hadn't returned. Heaving a disappointed sigh, she spritzed the final spot and wiped it. She was about to go inside when the red truck drove up.

"You hire out?" Ross called playfully. "My windows could stand some help."

She smiled. "No, but I'll loan you the cleaner and paper towels."

"That's no deal." Laughing, he let down the tailgate and hefted several lengths of shelving from the bed.

Entranced, she watched the muscles on his arms and back flex as he held the lumber aloft and balanced it on his head. His shirt went higher and his pants went lower. Once again, she grew fascinated with his navel and the sprinkle of dark hair that grew just below it.

She clutched the spray bottle to her bosom as her gaze followed his loose-hipped gait to the door of his town house. He hesitated there and said something she didn't catch.

"Susan, I've got a problem," he called out a moment later. "Could you give me a hand with the door?"

"Sure." She hurried over and tried to yank it open. It didn't budge.

"It's locked. The keys are in my pocket."

Her breath caught. "Your pocket?"

"Yeah. The right one I think. Do you mind?"

"Of course not," she said, trying to keep her voice normal and her manner blasé. She stepped behind him and gingerly eased her fingers into his jeans pocket. His nearness, his masculine scent assailed her senses. She held her breath, trying not to think of muscle and sinew and . . . other masculine accoutrements, as her hand slipped deeper into the warmth of his pocket.

A relieved whoosh of air escaped her when she felt keys. She snatched them out and jingled them in front of his face. "Got 'em."

"Those are my truck keys, doll. Try again."

Her hand slipped back into his pocket. Though it was a balmy day in late October and the temperature couldn't have been more than seventy-five degrees, Susan's forehead and upper lip grew decidedly damp.

She found sixty-eight cents in change, a gasoline receipt, and a spearmint gum wrapper, but no other keys.

"Try the left pocket," he said.

She swiped her forehead, switched the glass cleaner to her other hand, and fished in his left pocket. Her fingers seemed to have grown new nerve endings. She could feel the weave of the fabric, the line of his shorts, the heat of his body. When he shifted his weight and the muscles of his upper thigh bunched under her hand, her finger automatically tightened on the trigger of the spray bottle.

He flinched. "What was that?"

Blue glass cleaner dribbled down his arm.

"Oops. Sorry. I squirted you by mistake." Feeling like a prize idiot with twelve thumbs, she quickly blotted his arm. Then, clenching her teeth, she plunged into the depths of his pocket once more and grabbed another set of keys. "Are these the ones?" she asked, jingling the second set for him to see.

"The big gold one."

Her hands were none too steady, but she managed to unlock the door and hold it open while he maneuvered his load inside.

"Thanks," he said, grinning and giving her a big wink.

"You're welcome. Now, if you'll excuse me—"

"Wait. One other thing." He leaned the shelving against a wall and walked back to her. "Since I'm new in town, I was hoping you might . . ." He propped his hand on the wall beside her head and leaned toward her.

He was so close, she could smell the spearmint gum on his breath, and he seemed very big as she looked up at him. Like no man she'd ever encountered before, Ross Berringer was overwhelmingly sexy . . . and a little scary. Well, a lot scary. A gorgeous fantasy man was one thing, the reality quite another. Her feet itched to run, but she bade them stay.

". . . recommend a good maid service."

Disappointment almost overwhelmed her. She stammered out some answer and escaped before she could make a complete fool of herself.

Ross stood at the door of his town house and watched Susan Sinclair hurry away. She was a hard one to figure. The first time he'd seen her, she'd looked as sexy as all get out in her little cotton skivvies—delightfully rumpled like a lush lady after a night of good loving. Yet, at the store she'd looked as prim and pristine as a Sunday School teacher. Her full lips alternated from exuding plum-ripe sensuality that begged for kissing to looking as if she'd sucked a green persimmon. One minute she was as nervous as a calf at branding time, the next she was bolder than a Brahma bull.

Even with her unflattering way of dressing she was attractive. But with her hair loose and a little paint on, she'd be a knockout. She was an enchanting little thing—well, maybe not so little except compared to him. He liked the deep dimple in her chin and the way her eyes tilted up at the corners. He'd always thought eyes told a lot about a person, and hers intrigued him. An odd combination of innocence and mysterious allure, their pale blue-gray shimmer reminded him of a distant summer rainstorm. Even her smell tantalized him—an unusual blend like delicate peach blossoms and heady Oriental spice.

Hell, he sounded like a damned poet. Shaking his head, he closed the door. What was it about Susan Sinclair that wriggled under his skin and teased his mind?

He'd gotten a kick out of her fumbling in his pockets. And it had affected him more than he'd let on. Had she been jittery because she was shy? Or had she felt the powerful attraction too?

He had a premonition that something potent was going to develop between the two of them. He'd been itching to ask her out, but he had a ton of work to catch up on in his new territory. Besides the usual tasks, he'd taken over his predecessor's investigation of a bank robbery and a murder case. He didn't know when he'd have any free time. He was lucky to have gotten a day off to move part of his belongings from Waco. Sometimes being a Texas Ranger wasn't all it was cracked up to be.

# Two

Susan hadn't seen Ross or his red pickup for several days. Every morning when she woke and peeked out the window, he'd been gone, and a couple of times she'd heard him drive in long after she was in bed reading.

Perhaps it was just as well she told herself; she was likely too ordinary for a man like him. He probably preferred glamorous women who could flirt and laugh and tease—like her own mother who knew how to charm and pander to a man's ego by acting helpless and dependent. Men adored her mother, as evidenced by five marriages and a long string of male admirers. But even if it meant being lonely, Susan was determined not to be like her. Her mother's emotionally flighty behavior had left its scars. Scars upon scars for as far back as she could remember. Deep scars that had only healed on the outside.

No, she probably wasn't Ross Berringer's type. And if attracting him meant becoming a simpering, self-absorbed woman like her mother, she'd pass, she thought bitterly.

But still she thought about him—a lot.

The store was quiet, and Susan, pushing thoughts of her mother aside and humming a nameless tune, wielded her feather duster over the techno-thriller section. When the bell on the front door sounded, she turned with her usual smile of greeting.

Her heart did a little jig.

It was *him*—Ross Berringer—grinning in that pulse-palpitating way of his and dressed very differently from the way he had the last time she'd seen him. The crisp white dress shirt he wore emphasized his dark good looks, while the rest of his clothes added a deliciously dangerous edge to his appearance: shiny black boots, black slacks, a black leather vest, and a black cowboy hat pulled low on his forehead and sporting a rattlesnake hatband, complete with rattles.

As he sauntered toward her, her breath quickened and she went warm all over. She tucked a nonexistent loose strand into her chignon and opened her mouth, gaping, she was sure, like a guppy, trying to think of something intelligent to say. After fiddling with the bow at the collar of her beige dress, she finally managed a mundane, "Hello."

He stopped very near her, and his grin widened as he shoved his hat back. "Hi, neighbor. How's it going?"

"Uh, great. Are you looking for a book?"

"Well, I guess I might look for a book, but mostly I stopped in to visit."

His answer sparked a glow inside her. She smiled. "I like your hat."

"Part of my sexy desperado look." His dark eyes twinkling with mischief, he took off the hat and shook it so that the rattles sounded. "It's designed to drive women wild. Did it work?"

*If he only knew*, she thought. *Or maybe he did.* She laughed. "I'll try to restrain myself."

He snapped his fingers and said, "Aw, shoot."

When he propped his elbow on the corner of the metal rack she'd been dusting, his vest rode up to expose an ominous-looking pearl-handled pistol on his belt. Her eyes widened. A thousand thoughts zipped through her mind. "You— you're wearing a gun."

"Yes, ma'am, it goes with the job."

"Are you a policeman?"

He drew his vest back to expose a silver star pinned to his shirt. "Texas Ranger."

She blinked at the star, then looked up at the handsome man who towered over her. "A Texas Ranger? For real?"

Laughing, he held his hat over his chest. "Sergeant Ross Berringer, Company A, at your service."

"How exciting! I don't think I've ever met a Ranger before. Do you have a horse?"

"My brother and I keep a few at our ranch near Giddings, but nowadays it's pretty hard to chase bank robbers on horseback when they're driving souped-up cars. You tend to lose them on the interstate."

Susan felt very foolish. "How silly of me. I was thinking of those rough, tough Rangers of the old west I've read about—the hard-riding, fast-shooting kind who rode into town and rustled up the outlaws single-handedly."

Ross resettled his hat low on his forehead, hung his thumbs in his belt, and gave her a cheeky grin. "Well, ma'am," he drawled, "I'm here to tell you that I'm rougher than a three-cornered cob and tougher than a two-bit steak. I can ride hard and shoot the whiskers off a gnat at a hundred yards—if the sun's not in my eyes. When outlaws see me coming, they tremble in their boots and light a shuck for the border."

She couldn't help laughing at his exaggerations. "You're outrageous."

His eyes widened in mock surprise. "Outrageous? Me?" He glanced around the store. "You don't see any outlaws lurking behind the shelves, do you, darlin'?"

"I don't think I've seen a single one today."

"See?" He grinned and tapped her nose with his index finger. "They must've heard I was coming."

"No doubt."

He hung one arm over the shelf and rested his other hand on his hip. "Say, I was wondering—" The beeper on his belt sounded before he could finish. "Duty calls at the damnedest times. May I use your phone?"

Susan busied herself while he was talking on the telephone and tried not to listen, but she gathered that Ross had to go somewhere and do something—pronto.

After he hung up, he ambled over to her and pushed his hat back. "Just when I thought I might get some breathing room, all hell breaks loose. I'll see you in a couple of days. Would you mind picking up my mail while I'm gone?"

She agreed and he left. She stood at the window and watched his pickup roar out of the lot. What had he been about to say before he was interrupted?

A few days later, Susan and Linda sat perched on stools behind the counter of The Great Escape, sharing brown-bag lunches. From their vantage point they had an excellent view inside the gym—and of the man working out.

"He is one gorgeous specimen." Linda Brewer sighed and took a bite from her sandwich, keeping her gaze on Ross as he pumped iron.

"He's a hunk all right," Susan agreed, reaching for a potato chip. Her eyes were glued to Ross, who was dressed in a skimpy tank top and even skimpier shorts. "He sort of reminds me of Tom Selleck without the mustache and with extra muscles."

"I've noticed him spending *lots* of time in the bookstore," Linda said. "Has he asked you out yet?"

"Nope. Living next door to each other, we've met a few times coming and going, and he's stepped inside the store several times to browse or buy or sometimes just to chat for a few minutes. I really like him. He has a terrific sense of humor, and he could charm the warts off a toad. Sometimes I'm sure he's interested; then other times I just don't know what's going on in his head. He's very friendly, and, Lord knows, I've given him every opening, but he hasn't—" She frowned. "Do you suppose he could be *married*?"

Linda rolled her eyes and slapped her hand

across her chest. "Perish the thought! What a waste."

Susan chewed and watched his delicious muscles bunch and bulge as he hoisted a weight. "No, I don't think he's married. At least he doesn't wear a ring, and I haven't seen a woman around his house. But maybe he has a girlfriend. Wouldn't that be the pits?" She nibbled on a pickle.

"The absolute pits."

"I guess I'm not his type." When Ross moved out of their range, Susan propped her chin in her hand, stared off into space, and sighed. "Do you ever find your life boring? Wouldn't you like to travel to exotic places or do wild, thrilling things?"

"I'm perfectly happy with Don and Beaumont, thank you." Linda laid her hand on Susan's arm. "But you're not happy, are you?"

"I'm restless. And it's been getting worse. Do you realize that I'll be thirty-two years old next month? And what do I have to show for it? *Nada.* I've always dreamed of leading a life of excitement and adventure and glamour, but about the most exciting thing that ever happened to me was when I got *tourista* on my honeymoon in Cancun. I'm tired of being ordinary, boring Susan Sinclair. Deep inside of me is a part that's aching to go places and do things before I'm too old to enjoy life. That part of me is rattling the cage to get out. I want to *do* something exciting instead of simply reading about it."

"Then why don't you cut loose and *do* it?"

"Because I . . . I don't know." She sighed. "It would be nice if I *were* Ross's type."

Linda stuffed the remains of her lunch into the trash. "What do you think his type is?"

"Oh, beautiful and sexy and . . . fluttery."

"I'll pass on the fluttery part," Linda said, "but if you'll give me a couple of hours I can have you rivaling Kim Bassinger."

"What do you mean?"

"I mean, friend, that you need a new hairdo—something kind of wild and manelike, I think. You need to update your makeup, too. Did you know that the sixties look is back in? With your beautiful eyes, extra liner would be smashing. And when was the last time you went shopping for new clothes?"

Susan felt her heart sink. "Am I that bad?"

Linda hugged her. "Of course not. You're very attractive. You always have been, but you need to play up your features instead of hiding them. I'd die for your cheekbones and your tall, curvy figure. You just rusticated too long in a moldy old library and with that wimp you married. A few changes on the outside will give you more confidence inside. If you're going duck hunting, you need camouflage. If you're going manhunting, you need to look the part, too."

Susan grimaced. "That sounds like my mother. She primps for two hours before she'll even go to the grocery store—in case she might run into an interesting man. I don't want to be like her."

Rolling her eyes, Linda said, "Give me a break. You're nothing like your mother. In fact, I think you bend over backwards to go to the other extreme. How are you going to have a love life or find a husband if you don't apply yourself a little?"

"I'm not looking for a husband. I tried it once,

remember? I don't intend to follow in my mother's footsteps. But I have a love life."

Linda snorted. "Surely you jest. I don't call a few evenings at the movies with that anemic looking IRS auditor a love life. And that ditzy history teacher you were seeing before him— ugh! Sometimes I think you deliberately pick the dullest men you can find just to be safe."

"I do not! How can you say such a thing?"

Linda shrugged. "Looks that way to me. I mean, who can really pour her heart into a relationship with a man who loves to run his fingers through 1040s or whose idea of a fun evening is to refight some Civil War battle with little tin soldiers? Did either of those dorks even kiss you?"

"Of course they kissed me."

"And? Did the earth move?"

Susan cleared the remnants of her lunch from the counter before she answered. "Not a leaf rustled."

"That's what I thought." Linda gave her a smug look. "I'll bet you wouldn't say that about him." She nodded toward Ross, who was headed for The Great Escape. "I'd bet this week's tips that he could really shake your tree."

A sudden knot of apprehension gripped Susan's middle. She shook it off and lifted her chin. "I'm really not interested in finding out."

"Susan Sinclair, you're lying through your teeth. You know darned well that he turns you on like crazy. You talk a good game, but I think that down deep the idea of getting involved with somebody like Ross scares the pants off you. He might stir some—God forbid—mindless passion in your soul. Why don't you come out from behind that wall you've built and shake your booty at a real man for a change?"

Sniffing, Susan replied, "Shaking my booty is not my style."

Linda wiggled her eyebrows and grinned. "It's a real kick. You ought to try it. I double-dog dare you."

The bell tinkled as Ross opened the door and stuck his head in. He flashed a big grin and said, "Are you two gals plotting the overthrow of the male population, or is it safe to ask if I could buy you lunch at Hebert's? I'll get take-out and bring it back here."

"Oh, we've—" Susan began, but Linda stepped squarely on her big toe and interrupted.

"Nothing for me, thanks," Linda said. "I have to get back to the shop, but I'll bet Susan would love a bowl of gumbo. Wouldn't you, Susan?" She gave her a nudge.

"A bowl of gumbo would be great," Susan agreed.

"I'll be back in half a shake," Ross said.

When he'd gone, Susan turned to her friend. "How do you think I'm going to eat a bowl of gumbo? I just finished lunch and I'm full."

"Susan, *honestly!* You have to learn to use a little guile. I've got to go, but anytime you decide to get a new look, I'll clear my appointment book for you."

After her friend left, Susan waited on a customer, then sat fidgeting at the counter. She hurriedly dashed on lipstick and smoothed her dress.

Time seemed to drag by. She drummed her fingers on the cash register, then straightened a stack of mail. With every second that passed, her heartbeat picked up.

At last Ross came through the door carrying a small sack. He was frowning. "Hon," he said, "sometimes crooks have the lousiest timing. I've got an emergency over in Orange." He held out the bag to her. "But I brought your gumbo. Catch you later, okay?"

He was out the door before she could respond. Well, she thought, so much for her shot at booty shaking.

That night she warmed the gumbo in the microwave and ate it for dinner. Alone.

Ross shifted his weight in the front seat of a state-issued gray sedan and kept his eyes on the house down the block. At two o'clock in the morning on a weeknight, nothing stirred but the wind in the oleander bushes.

He'd rather be doing almost anything other than stakeouts. Just when he thought that his work load had leveled off and he could ask Susan out, he'd been stuck with watching an escaped convict's mother's house. He'd pulled the night shift for the past three days. He hadn't even seen Susan in all that time. But he'd thought about her—often. Something about her tugged at his heart. At the strangest times, he remembered her smell, her smile, her lush lips, and he ached to touch her and taste her. He'd a hell of a lot rather be snuggled up with a sweet-smelling woman than sitting here getting cal-luses on his butt. He couldn't believe that he'd found a lady who really interested him and his schedule was so crazy that he couldn't even spend an evening with her.

Of the few things he hated about being a Texas Ranger, waiting topped the list. He didn't have his twin brother Holt's patience. Holt was a Ranger, too, stationed in Austin. The pair of them had always been a matched set; they'd done everything together—until Holt up and got married a few months before. Ross had never thought much about settling down with one woman himself, but he admitted that he'd had a niggle or two in the last few weeks. Maybe seeing how happy his brother and his wife, Cory, were had put the idea in his head.

In his own way, Ross was as dedicated to Rangering as his brother, although he chafed against authority more than Holt. Ross was more of a maverick, but from the time the twins were knee high to jackrabbits, they'd planned on becoming Rangers like their grandpa and ancestors from several generations before them. It was a family tradition. Sometimes, like now, the tradition weighed very heavily on his mind.

Lord, he despised surveillance. It was life wasted.

"Probably a damned wild goose chase," he muttered.

Down the street, something darted around the bushes of the house he watched. Ross sat up. A couple of minutes later, a light went on in a back room, then the porch light flashed on briefly. The few moments of illumination were enough for him to see what could be the hulking shape of Melvin P. Yarborough.

Ross grinned and picked up the mike of his

radio. With any luck, Melvin would soon be back serving out his life sentence, and Ross could have some free time of his own. He wondered if Susan liked to dance.

A few minutes before closing time, Susan rang up the Cliff Notes that a teenage boy had selected. "Thank you," she said, handing him the sack. "Come again."

She glanced up to see Ross entering as the boy left. With his usual black hat, he wore a blue chambray shirt and well-worn jeans that hugged his muscular thighs like shrink-wrap. As it did every time he came near, her heart lurched.

"Well, hello," she said. "I haven't seen you in a while."

"Miss me?" He grinned. She blushed. "It took me a while to get my man," he told her, "but I got him."

"Do you always get your man?" *Or woman?* she added silently.

"You betcha. I'm a persistent cuss." As he leaned against the counter, his gaze passed over her appreciatively. "Say, I like your hair down." He reached out and toyed with a curl that brushed her shoulder.

"Thanks." Two days before, she'd succumbed to Linda's prodding and changed to the more fashionable style that Linda had insisted on. It was a bit wild and manelike, but not nearly as extreme as her friend had wanted. Everyone had complimented her new look. Still well below her shoulders, her thick tresses had been layered for softness around her face and highlighted with paler streaks. Each time she passed by a mirror, she did a double take at the reflection she saw. She hadn't worn her hair down in years, but she liked the way it felt. Loose. Sensual. She liked the extra makeup she'd tried, Linda insisted it lent her a mysterious allure.

She'd even gone shopping for a few new outfits, such as the green silk tunic and the sleek black pants she was wearing. The bright colors and marvelous-to-the-touch fabrics felt a little decadent, but delicious.

Not that she'd made any of the changes to snare Ross. Her new look was totally for her, but still it warmed her when he said, "You look good enough to eat," as his gaze slid over the contours of her blouse like a palpable caress. "And speaking of eating, are you about through for the day?"

"Don't I wish. After I close the store tonight, I have several hours of work to do in the back room."

"The back room?" His eyes crinkled into dark half moons, and his mouth curved into a suggestive smile. "Don't tell me you have one of those 'Joe sent me' places in the rear."

She laughed. "Hardly. I have a month's worth of paperwork to do in my office. Very boring bookkeeping duties. I always put them off as long as I can."

He leaned even closer and laid his hand over hers. His thumb absently stroked her wrist. "Need some help? I'm pretty good with back room stuff, and my services are cheap."

Her heart kicked into overdrive. Her imagination went berserk. What was he offering? His tone hinted at more than adding columns of figures. She'd been fantasizing about him for days, conjuring up all sorts of sexy scenarios between the two of them, but now that he seemed to be moving in, she wasn't sure that they were in the same league. She didn't know how to handle a man like Ross. She felt a moment of panic, and, when the phone rang, she jerked her hand away, grateful for the distraction.

Grabbing the receiver, she answered, "Great Escape." Her grandmother's voice came on the line. "Slow down, Dagna. I can't understand you. Are you all right?"

Her grandmother repeated the distraught message.

"Stay calm. I'll close the store and be there as soon as I can." Her hand shaking, she hung up the phone and turned to Ross. "My grandmother has had an emergency. I have to go."

Frantic with worry, she dashed to the rear office for her purse and keys. She fumbled with her purse and dropped her keys twice on her way back to the front. Ross still stood by the counter.

"Is there something I can do to help?" he asked.

"No, thanks." She tried to open the register to remove the day's receipts, but her hands were shaking so badly that she kept hitting the wrong buttons.

"Here, let me do that, sugar." Ross gently moved her aside and opened the cash drawer. "What do you want to do with the money?"

Susan grabbed a zippered bag from under the counter. "Put it all in here."

He took the bag, quickly transferred the bills

into it, and stuck it under his arm. With his hand under her elbow guiding her, he turned off the store lights and locked the door on their way out.

She started toward her sports car, but he steered her in another direction. She stopped and jerked away. "What are you doing? I have to get to Dagna's immediately."

"Sweetheart, you're in no condition to drive. You're shaking like a treed kitten," he said gently. "I'll take you where you need to go."

"But—"

"No arguments, Susan."

Something in his tone convinced her that any argument would be futile. Like a man on a critical mission, he took charge and bulldozed her toward his truck. He tossed the money bag onto the seat and helped her inside the cab.

When he was behind the wheel, he quickly started the truck and said, "Where to?"

"Vendor. It's a little town about fifteen miles north of here on Highway two-eighty-seven."

He spun out of the lot and headed north.

"Take a few deep breaths," he told her.

She did. It helped only marginally. "I'm sorry I'm being such a nuisance. Usually I'm very calm in a crisis, but I don't know what I'd do if something happened to Dagna. She practically raised me."

"Is Dagna your grandmother?"

"Yes. My mother's mother. When I was a baby the closest I could get to saying 'Grandmother' was 'Dagna.' It stuck."

"Did you lose your folks?"

Susan laughed. "More like they lost me."

"How could they lose you?"

"In the shuffle, I suppose. You'd have to know my mother. She's a charming scatterbrain who goes through husbands like tissues. Mother usually parked me with Dagna when she was between husbands or involved with a *significant other*, which was often. Mother adores men, but she has a short attention span. My father was her second husband, and now she's in Bermuda on her honeymoon with husband number five. Or is it six? I can't always keep up."

"What about your father?"

"Oh, I haven't seen him since I was four. He's a cardiologist in St. Louis, and he has another wife and family now. I guess he knows where I am since he sends me a Christmas card every year. Or rather his office does. It's always one of these fancy foil numbers with 'Avril M. Sinclair, M.D.' printed at the bottom after the verse."

"Do you have any brothers or sisters?"

"An assorted bunch of stepsisters and stepbrothers and one half-brother who's a lot older. I'm not close to any of them." Frowning, Susan turned to study Ross. "Are you really interested in my life story, or are you trying to keep my mind off Dagna?"

He chuckled. "Both."

"Thanks. I'm okay now, really. Calm as a clam." She held out her hand to show him it was steady. "What about your family?"

Raindrops splattered on the windshield, and Ross turned on the wipers. "Pretty ordinary by comparison," he said. "One father, deceased, one mother still going strong, two brothers. What's the emergency I'm breaking the speed limit for?"

"Dagna broke her hip, and she's alone."

"Is she in the hospital?"

"No, I don't mean she broke it today. It happened about three weeks ago when she was sweeping pine needles off her roof. Can you believe a seventy-nine year old woman on the roof? I've told her a dozen times to slow down, but she's an independent soul. Anyway, Mother hired a live-in companion to stay with Dagna until her hip heals. The companion has disappeared."

"Disappeared?"

"That's what Dagna says. Maureen went to the grocery store several hours ago and hasn't returned. I don't know any more than that. My grandmother was very upset."

"Maybe she had car trouble or an accident. The weather's right for it. It looks like we're running into a storm."

Rain beat against the truck as they sped down the highway. Ross turned the wipers on high and peered through the downpour from the darkening sky. They were quiet as he concentrated on the highway, and Susan agonized about Dagna alone and helpless in bed.

"I should have called a neighbor to stay with Dagna until I could get there."

Ross reached across and patted her thigh. "Don't fret about it, sugar. I'll have you there in a couple of minutes. She's going to be fine, just fine." He stroked her thigh and patted it again.

Her hand covered his, and she clutched it like a lifeline. His touch warmed her, comforted her. Yet, at the same time, it disquieted her. His hand, broad with long fingers that were dark against the lighter shade of hers, radiated a strength that seeped into her skin. The intimacy stirred other feelings in her as well, potent feelings of sexual awareness.

His thumb absently stroked her thigh, and she grew warmer and squirmed in her seat. She chastised herself for concentrating on the man at the wheel instead of her grandmother, but his presence couldn't be ignored. Ross seemed to have electricity in his fingers. Her skin zinged like a high voltage wire, and her heart hammered so hard she could feel the pounding in her throat.

His presence seemed to expand and expand until the cab pulsated with his muscular aura. She remembered her hand in his pocket and the feel of his thigh against her fingers. Did he have the same awareness touching her? She squirmed again, but she continued to hang on to his hand.

He smiled at her and squeezed her leg. "Don't worry, hon. We're almost there."

When she spotted a road sign that read: Vendor City Limits, Population 2612, she breathed a relieved sigh. "Turn right at the light."

She directed him through a series of turns until he was in the driveway of a rambling white house with "Bendel" on the mailbox.

"Dagna's car is still missing," she said. "Pull into the carport so we don't get soaked."

Before the pickup's motor died, she jumped from the cab and dashed in through the kitchen door. With Ross's heavy boots clomping on the hardwood floors behind her, she ran through the rooms of the familiar old house filled with Victorian furniture until she was in the large front bedroom that belonged to her grandmother.

"Dagna," she cried, "are you all right?"

Her grandmother, dressed in a pink bed jacket and with her white hair in a neat knot atop her head, lay propped up in bed with the TV blaring the evening news.

Dagna's weathered, lined face screwed into a scowl. "Well, of course I'm not all right. I'm madder than blue blazes. That good for nothing Maureen Potts that your mother hired has been gone since ten o'clock this morning. She left to make a quick trip to the grocery store and to the drugstore for my medicine, and I haven't seen her since. I couldn't even reach my walker to get up and fix my own lunch. My stomach would have stuck to my backbone if it hadn't been for that box of chocolate-covered cherries you brought me last Sunday. My rump's fair worn out and my bladder is about to pop from being stuck in this bed. You mark my words, that hussy—" She stopped her diatribe and peered over Susan's shoulder. "And who are you, young man?"

Susan glanced back at Ross, who stood lounging against the doorjamb grinning. He picked up the folded walker in the hall, ambled into the room, swept off his hat, and bowed to the old lady who was giving him the once over.

"Ross is my name, ma'am. A friend come to your rescue." He unfolded the walker and set it beside her bed, then leaned over and kissed her wrinkled forehead. "Don't you worry about a thing, ma'am. We'll get it all straightened out quicker than a New York minute. While Susan helps you here, I'll rustle up some grub."

After he'd gone, Susan helped Dagna to the bathroom, then resettled her in bed.

"What was that star pinned to your young man's shirt?" Dagna asked.

"He's a Texas Ranger."

"A Ranger? Well, I swan. Your granddaddy once wanted to become a Texas Ranger."

"I didn't know that. Why didn't he?"

"Because he couldn't ride a horse worth a flip. He never did get along with four-legged critters, except for his coon dogs. Is Ross your new beau?" Dagna asked.

"Oh, no. He's just a friend. He lives next door."

"You ought to grab on to him, honey. He's a fine figure of a fellow. Reminds me a little of your granddaddy, except he's taller. He's certainly a sight better than that pantywaist you picked the first time. This one is a real man. Never did understand what you saw in Thomas Rowe. I was beginning to fear that you might not have any better judgment about men than your mother."

"Who's Thomas Rowe?" Ross asked as he strode into the room bearing a tray.

Susan started and flushed at the thought that he'd overheard. "Here, let me help you." She reached for the tray.

"I can manage." He settled the tray across Dagna's lap, flicked open a napkin and tucked it under her chin. "Best I could do on short notice," he said, indicating the bowl of tomato soup, beautifully toasted grilled cheese sandwich, and milk. He grinned. "I figured you've already had your dessert."

Dagna laughed. "I like a sense of humor in a man." She took a few bites of food, then looked up at Ross. "Good looking devil and you can cook, too. You'll do."

"Who's Thomas Rowe?" he asked.

Before her grandmother could answer, Susan asked, "Dagna, have you called the police to see if Maureen had an accident?"

"No need. Everybody in town knows my car. Leonard would have called me."

"Who's Leonard?" Ross asked.

"Leonard Bottoms, the chief of police. Hasn't got the sense God gave a billy goat." Dagna drank the last of her milk and blotted her lips. "Very tasty, young man. That hit the spot."

"Did you call the grocery store to see if she'd been by?" Susan asked.

Dagna nodded curtly. "Talked to Henry Gears at the supermarket and Winston Moncrief at the pharmacy. Neither one of them has seen hide nor hair of her. She probably met up with some man and is shacked up at the Shady Rest Motel. Or she's lit out with my car. I never did trust a woman with two-toned hair."

"Two-toned hair?" Ross asked.

"It was growing out from being bleached," Susan explained.

"About a year's worth of growth," Dagna added. "I figure she'd been in the pokey about that long."

"Now, Dagna, you know Mother checked her references from the health service."

"Barbara was more interested in marrying that idiot with the bad toupee than she was in checking references. I told her that Essie could have come and stayed with me, but she wanted somebody with *nursing* experience. Why, Essie has nursed seven kids and eighteen grandkids."

"Ladies," Ross said, "I think we need to focus on the present situation. Either something has delayed Maureen or she's left deliberately. Susan, why don't you check her room to see if her things are missing?"

# *Three*

Susan hurried to the bedroom next to Dagna's and checked the closet and bureau drawers. Fury made her teeth clench as she quickly checked the sideboard. She stalked back into Dagna's room.

"Her clothes are gone. And so is the silver."

The silver wasn't the only thing that had disappeared. Dagna's purse had been rifled, they discovered, and her cash, credit cards, identification, and checkbook were missing. Gone too was the velvet box that held Dagna's good jewelry—a diamond and platinum brooch with matching earrings, three diamond rings, two strings of pearls, pearl ear clips, and a black opal stickpin.

"That opal stickpin was the last present your granddaddy gave me before he died." Tears glazed the old woman's eyes, but she blinked them away. "No wonder that hussy was so anxious that I take my sleeping pills last night. *I* wanted to watch Arsenio Hall, but she insisted that I needed my rest. Humph! She was antsy to get on with her looting. She'd probably have carted off my bed if I hadn't been in it. Susan, you and your young man go through the house and make a list of everything that green-eyed polecat made off with while I call Leonard Bottoms—though I don't expect any help from him. That man couldn't find his nose in the dark. Never was one of the Bottoms bunch that had a lick of sense. Don't forget to check the gun case and the coin collection. And my grandmother's crystal inkwell."

The inkwell sat in its customary place on the rolltop desk, but the gun case was empty and the coins were gone. By the time Susan and Ross entered the kitchen, the list of missing items filled a page in the notebook Susan carried.

"The microwave I gave her last Christmas is gone. So is the portable TV that always sat here." She patted an empty space on the counter. A terrible sick feeling filled her and clutched at her throat. She tossed the notebook aside and leaned her forehead against the refrigerator, fighting the tears that stung her eyes. "Oh, Ross, how could anyone rip off a helpless old lady?"

He gathered her into his arms and held her close, stroking her back and swaying her gently. "I don't know, sugar. I don't know. But don't you worry, we'll catch her."

"How are we going to catch her? She could be anywhere."

"We'll find her. Don't you worry."

He continued to hold her, and she closed her eyes and snuggled closer against his muscled strength, drawing comfort from his massive size and confident words. Being in his arms was like being enfolded by an oak tree. He nuzzled the top of her head with his cheek, and his breath stirred her hair and warmed her scalp. Beneath her hand that was splayed across his chest, she could feel the strong, steady beat of his heart.

As they stood together in the old-fashioned kitchen where the smells of pine cleaner, recently grilled bread, and the faint memories of thousands of meals scented the air, only the sound of rain pounding the windows and their breathing interrupted the quiet. She knew she should break away and continue her inventory, but being in his arms felt so good, so right that she lingered, nestled her head under his cheek, and sighed.

He seemed content to hold her as well. He kissed her hair again and stroked her back from shoulders to waist and back again. Her palm smoothed a circle over his broad chest, marveling at the taut muscles she touched. Her little finger slid through the placket of his shirt and met skin and a downy patch of hair. Fascinated, and without thinking, she slipped three buttons open and her hand slithered inside to explore his bare chest. His heartbeat increased in tempo and his hand dipped below her waist to scoop her hips closer to him.

Her hand stilled. She leaned back and looked up at him. His eyes gleamed midnight black. She licked her lips, and his nostrils flared.

"I think I'm gonna have to kiss you, Sin." His voice was deep and provocative.

She sighed. "Oh, Lord, I hope so."

He chuckled and his head dipped. His lips were soft and gentle as his mouth moved against hers in a slow seduction. His tongue teased inside to touch hers, and his hands glided along her back in a leisurely stroke that turned her body into warm wax. She moaned in satisfaction, circled his neck with her arms, and, tiptoeing, kneaded herself against him, wanting to mold her body into his. She tugged at his shirt and ran her hands over the bare flesh of his rock-solid torso.

His lips left hers, and his powerful arms cradled her bottom and lifted her until they were face to face. His eyes, black and heavy lidded, closed, and he drew in a deep breath through his nostrils. "Hooo-wee, Sin," he said, laughing softly. "You're full of surprises."

Languidly, he undulated his solid frame and rolled her against him until she melted into the angles and contours of his substantial form. She could feel the buttons on his shirt, his buckle, his growing hardness.

She gasped, then her mouth went slack with delicious sensation. The tip of his tongue traced the curve of her lower lip with maddening slowness, before his mouth at last moved over hers again. Never had she been kissed as Ross was kissing her. Her whole body felt as if it had expanded. Her belly quivered. Bells went off in her head.

When he tried to pull back, she whimpered and her mouth followed his, loathe to break contact.

"Babe," he whispered, dropping soft, quick kisses on the corners of her mouth, "I think I heard the telephone, and someone's at the door."

Totally engulfed in their intimate activity, she drifted in a surreal fog. "Tell them to go away."

"It's probably the police."

When the reality of the situation crashed through her hedonistic daze, she stiffened and her eyes widened. "Dagna. Leonard Bottoms. How could I have forgotten?" She wiggled in his arms.

Setting her on her feet, he brushed her lips with his finger. "We'll finish this later."

Susan rushed to the door to find the police chief standing on the porch, rain dripping from his hat. Embarrassment flushed her face. "Please come in, Chief Bottoms. Sorry to keep you waiting. I was . . . uh, in the back of the house, and I didn't hear the door."

"No problem." The balding man with wire-rimmed glasses and a pot belly shed his slicker and hat, hung them on the hall tree, and wiped his booted feet on the hall runner. He took off his glasses and dried them with a handkerchief from his back pocket. "Mrs. Bendel says you've had some trouble."

"That you, Leonard?" Dagna called from her bedroom.

"Yes, ma'am."

Susan ushered the policeman to her grandmother's bedside, and Ross joined them.

"What seems to be the trouble, Mrs. Bendel?"

"I already told you what the trouble is, Leonard," Dagna said, her blue eyes snapping. "Maureen Potts has stolen everything around here that wasn't nailed down, then skipped town. I thought she looked bleary eyed this morning.

Must've worked all night loading up stuff. I'd bet my bottom dollar that she had an accomplice too."

Susan, Dagna, and Ross filled in the chief with their discoveries about the missing items, and Susan handed him the list. "That's only a preliminary inventory," she told him.

"Looks like quite a haul," the chief said.

"I want to know what you're going to do about it, Leonard," Dagna said.

"Well, I guess I can put out a bulletin on your car. A yellow seventy-three Cadillac shouldn't be hard to spot. Not too many of them left around. Most of them have been in the junkyard for years."

"I'll have you know, Leonard Bottoms, that car runs as good as it ever did," Dagna snapped. "Anyhow, that won't help you find her. Henry Gears from the grocery store just called. He was about to lock up when he saw my car sitting in the parking lot. One of his sack boys told him it had been there all afternoon. I told you she had an accomplice. They must have switched everything to another car, and she ditched mine at the supermarket."

Leonard swiped a hand across his bald head, then hung his thumb in his belt. "Well, that complicates things a mite. Don't suppose you have an address for her?"

"Are you loco, Leonard Bottoms? No, I don't have her address, and if I did, it would be phony. I don't have her driver's license or social security numbers either. My daughter Barbara was the one who hired her, and she's off gallivanting on her honeymoon with that screwball with the bad toupee. They're on a yacht somewhere around Bermuda. I don't even know how to get in touch with her."

Leonard shifted his weight from one foot to the other and looked perplexed. "She ever talk about any of her people?"

"I think she had a daughter somewhere around Waxahachie. Mary Alice, I think she called her," Dagna replied. "But I don't know her married name."

Chief Bottoms took a description of Maureen and the list of missing items. "Not much to go on, but we'll get right on it, Mrs. Bendel. Gonna be hard to track down, though, without any kind of I.D."

Ross cleared his throat. "Chief Bottoms, I'm Ross Berringer, a Texas Ranger out of Beaumont. I just came along because I'm a friend of Susan's, but I'll be glad to help out any way I can. You need any assistance in dusting for fingerprints?"

"Fingerprints. That's a good idea, son." Leonard squinted through his glasses at Ross. "We'll get on that first thing in the morning. I'll be much obliged for your help." The chief hitched up his pants. "Well, I'd better be going. When you called, Martha put my dinner in the oven to keep warm. Roast beef and mashed potatoes," he said, patting his pot belly. "My favorite meal."

Disgusted with Leonard Bottom's preoccupation with his stomach rather than the theft, Susan started to see the chief to the door. Ross stopped her.

"Why don't you keep your grandmother company, sugar, and I'll walk Chief Bottoms out," he said, smiling down at her. "Maybe he'll want to take something with him from Maureen's room that's likely to have her fingerprints on it."

"Good idea, son. Good idea."

The two men left and Susan could hear the low rumble of their voices in the bedroom next door. A few minutes later, Ross came back into the room.

"Susan, I know you're going to want to stay with your grandmother tonight, but I need to get back to Beaumont. I don't want you to be without transportation, so I'm going to leave my truck for you." He handed her the keys. "The chief says there's a bus leaving in a few minutes, and I'm going to hitch a ride to the station with him. If it's okay with you, I can pick up your car and bring it to you in the morning."

"I hate to put you to so much trouble," she said.

"Shoot, sugar, it's no trouble. I don't mind a bit." After Susan gave him her keys, he ambled over to Dagna's bed and kissed the old lady's wrinkled cheek. "Now you stay out of trouble till I get back, you hear? When you get better, we'll go dancin'." He grinned and winked at her.

Dagna seemed to fight a smile, then beamed up at him. "Oh, get out of here, you rascal."

Laughing, he turned to Susan. "Anything you need for me to do? What about the bookstore?"

"I'll call Nadine to open the store, but would you feed my turtles?"

"Your turtles?"

She nodded. "Bond and Moneypenny. The key to my town house is on the ring." She walked him to the door where Leonard was pulling on his slicker. "It's still pouring outside," she said to Ross. "You'll get soaked."

"Shoot, sugar, I won't melt." He tweaked her nose. "I'll see you tomorrow."

By the time Ross let himself into Susan's house, it was well after midnight. He'd hung around the police station and waited until Bottoms had his dinner so that Ross could gently make suggestions for the investigation and supervise dusting the glass they'd taken from Maureen Potts's bedroom as well as the old yellow Caddy. They'd gotten some good prints for their files.

Susan's place had the same layout as his, but the similarity stopped there. Hers was filled with all the trappings of a home in a mixture of styles—all comfortable looking and colorful. She had nice pictures on the wall, lots of plants, and tons of books in the bookcases. It even smelled pretty—like her, a blend of delicate peach blossoms and sexy Oriental spice. His furniture was still in his apartment in Waco, and he'd had to rent stuff to make the place livable—a bed, a couch, a TV, and a kitchen table with two chairs. He had tons of books, too, but half of the few he'd moved with him were still in the cartons. He wouldn't be able to get the rest of his things until he had more free time.

He found the turtles' food and fed the two ugly green things with red spots on the side of their striped heads. He'd read somewhere once that people usually picked pets that looked like them. He squatted down and looked into the aquarium where one turtle swam and the other sat on one of the rocks protruding from the water. He didn't see a damned thing in either one of them that favored Susan.

"Bond and Moneypenny?" He chuckled at the names she'd given them. Why not Bond and Octopussy? And what was there to like about turtles? He'd rather have a dog or a horse. Or even a cat. He kind of admired cats. They were independent and went where they pleased, when they pleased, and didn't answer to anybody. That probably told a lot about him, he thought. A renegade all his life, he'd gotten his tail in a crack with his superiors a time or two for his independent ways. He wasn't the die-hard, by-the-book Ranger that his brother Holt was, but he always got the job done.

He stood and wandered around the room, looking through her books, noticing the mess she'd made of the newspaper she'd left on the couch and the half-empty mug of coffee on the table beside it. He wasn't very neat himself. Not that her place was messy. It simply had a lived-in look that he liked.

He strolled over to the corner where a fancy computer stood. It was a new top-of-the-line model with a modem and a laser printer. She even had a fax machine beside the desk. Was she some kind of computer nut? It occurred to him that, as fast as he was becoming involved with her, he really didn't know much about Susan Sinclair. He meant to remedy the situation—soon.

Once next door in his own place, he shed his clothes, showered, fell into bed, and thought some more about Susan. Lordamighty, kissing her had turned him inside out. In two minutes with her, he'd gotten more aroused than a rutting bull. What would have happened if they hadn't been interrupted?

He grinned in the darkness. He could hardly wait to get a hold of her again.

Just as Susan put the last of the breakfast dishes in the dishwasher, the doorbell rang. She wiped her hands on the thighs of a faded navy sweat suit she'd found in her old room and headed for the front of the house. When she opened the door, she found Ross standing on the porch. He was dressed in jeans, denim jacket, and boots, and wore his black cowboy hat pulled low on his forehead, but he shoved it back and grinned at her.

"Good morning, lil' darlin'. Did you miss me?" He kissed her softly.

"Ummm," she said, savoring the taste of him. "Why are you here so early?"

"I thought you might want your own car." He dangled her keys.

"Thanks." She stepped back. "Come in."

"Susan," Dagna called. "Was that somebody at the door?"

"It's me, sweetheart," he said loudly. "Ross. I thought I'd see if you were up to dancin' yet." He threw his arm around Susan and led her toward Dagna's bedroom.

Dagna was chuckling as they entered the room. "Not yet," she said. "But give me a couple more weeks, and I'll take you up on it."

"I was about to go pick up Essie," Susan told him. "She's agreed to stay with Dagna until she's able to get around on her own."

"Who's Essie?" he asked. "Is she trustworthy?"

"Humph!" replied Dagna. "A sight more trustworthy than that Maureen Potts, my daughter, dug up. If my Barbara had let me have my way in the first place, we wouldn't be in this mess now. Essie Waters was my housekeeper for twenty-seven years—and would be still if her kids hadn't insisted that she retire last year. She jumped at the chance to come over here. Watching soap operas and staring at four walls get mighty old, let me tell you."

"Sounds like you'll be in good hands," Ross said. "Why don't I keep you company while Susan fetches her?" He picked up a pack of cards from the nightstand and drew up a chair beside the bed. "Darlin', do you play gin rummy?"

"I can beat the socks off you, young man. Any day of the week."

Smiling, Susan left to the sound of riffling cards.

When she returned with Essie, the gin game was still in progress.

"After Essie had been introduced and she'd left to put her things away, Ross said, "Your grandmother is a card shark. I'm down twenty-three dollars." He grinned up at Susan and wiggled his eyebrows. "But I know all your secrets. I don't care much for Thomas Rowe either."

Susan felt a flush rise to her face. "Oh? Dagna, what have you been telling him?"

"Now, don't get in an uproar, Sin. I wormed it out of her." He kissed Dagna's cheek. "I gotta split, sweetheart, but I'll be back to see you." He peeled several bills from a money clip and handed them to the old lady.

"Dagna! Surely you're not going to take his money," Susan said.

"I *certainly* am. It'll teach him not to under-estimate an old lady."

Ross hooted with laughter.

When Susan walked him to the door, he asked, "When are you coming back to Beau-mont?"

"Later today or tonight. Maybe early tomorrow morning. I need to run errands for Dagna, and I need to cancel her credit cards. And I have a couple of ideas—leads I want to follow up."

He frowned. "What kind of leads?"

"I think it's strange that all of Dagna's monthly bills are missing. If Maureen took them, why?"

"She'd probably been charging stuff to your grandmother's accounts. When you call to can-cel the cards, explain the situation and have everyone issue a new statement. But, sugar, leave the leads to the professionals."

"Leonard Bottoms, a professional? If we count on him to recover the goods, we'll never see them. The man's incompetent. When I called Henry Gears at the supermarket this morning, Leonard hadn't even questioned him yet."

"Still, I don't want you messing with some-thing that might get you in over your head." He kissed the tip of her nose. "I'll keep an eye on things."

Blood started to boil in her toes and rose upward. Her eyes narrowed. "Over my head?"

"Hon, these folks may be dangerous. I just don't want you to get hurt. Leave this to the fellows who are trained for this type of work.

Don't worry your sweet little self about it one bit."

"Ross, I'm not a brainless imbecile. And I certainly have more savvy than Leonard Bottoms. I could probably find Maureen Potts while the chief is still picking his dinner from his teeth. The man is a joke."

"Just be patient. We'll find the woman, but these things take time."

"But—"

"I know it's aggravating, but you're a sensible lady." He kissed her. "Be reasonable and stay out of it."

After Ross left, Susan leaned against the door, savoring the taste of him.

*Sensible*, he'd called her. All her life she'd been labeled *sensible.* She hated being proper and reasonable and *sensible.* It was boring, boring, boring. Despite Dagna's loss, the last eighteen hours had been kind of exciting. The adrenaline high was exhilarating. And Ross . . . well, kissing Ross Berringer had pumped at least an extra gallon of adrenaline into her bloodstream. Simply thinking about him set her heart racing.

Then her eyes narrowed, and she drew herself up stiffly. *Don't worry your sweet little self about it one bit*, he'd said. Did he think she was a helpless piece of fluff like her mother? Well, she wasn't. Not by a long shot. She'd read thousands of mysteries, and she hadn't spent seven years as a research librarian for nothing. "Over my head, huh? Well, we'll just see about that."

She went to the kitchen for a pair of rubber gloves and headed for the garage.

# *Four*

Susan wrinkled her nose and started sifting through the contents of the first bag of garbage, putting the sorted stuff into a clean trash bag. It wasn't a pleasant job, but she'd read enough spy novels to know that garbage could provide a wealth of information. Nobody else had thought of it. Not Ross, and *certainly* not Leonard Bottoms.

Her ingenuity paid off. Among the chicken bones, soggy newspapers, fermenting banana peels, and various other malodorous remnants of daily living, she found Dagna's missing bills, including the one from the telephone company. She set aside the envelopes, smelly and stained by coffee grounds, and continued her rummaging.

In the depths of the second bag, she discovered a matchbook from a bar in Port Arthur. It hardly seemed likely that her grandmother had frequented such a place. Her heart pounded as she drew back the cover of the packet, hoping that she'd find a betraying telephone number scrawled inside. Instead she saw two bent matches and a picture of an extremely busty nude lady.

She also found a swizzle stick decorated with a miniature plastic spur from Slippery Sam's Saloon in Big D, a receipt from a dress shop in Groves, a small town adjacent to Port Arthur, and several empty prescription bottles. Most of the medicine was Dagna's and had come from the Vendor Pharmacy, but one looked suspicious. She wiped sticky red stuff from the small brown vial. Half the label was gone, including—wouldn't you just know it—the person's name, except for what might be an "o" and what was definitely an "n." Enough of the drug store's name and phone number remained for her to recognize that the pharmacy was part of a popular national chain, and the prescription number was intact.

After careful sorting, she spotted nothing else that seemed helpful, so she retied the bags, gathered her find, and took the items into the kitchen. She spread a newspaper on the table and dumped her discoveries in the middle of it.

Essie, who was chopping vegetables at the sink, screwed up her nose and wiped her hands on the apron tied around her considerable girth. "Child, what kind of smelly garbage are you bringing into my kitchen?"

Unintimidated by the affectionate scolding, Susan grinned at the aging woman who had been a second grandmother to her for as far back as she could remember. "This isn't garbage, Essie. These are clues."

"Clues? Humph. Smells like garbage to me.

And you don't smell none too sweet yourself, missy."

"But you love me anyway, don't you?" Laughing, she bussed Essie's dark cheek as she reached across the woman for a length of paper towel and dampened it. "I'm going to find Maureen Potts and get Dagna's stuff back."

"And just how do you plan to do that?"

"Logically and doggedly. Like Edward X. Delaney."

Essie frowned. "Edward who?"

"Edward X. Delaney, an absolutely brilliant fictional detective created by Lawrence Sanders," Susan said as she wiped the things she'd brought inside.

"You mean somebody from one of those books you've always got your nose stuck in?"

"Yep."

Essie shook her head and went back to chopping onions and carrots, mumbling something about "some folks and their crazy ideas."

Susan blotted the somewhat cleaner articles with a paper towel and sprayed them with a deodorizing disinfectant. After she'd tidied up the kitchen table, she opened the damp telephone bill and scanned its contents. A broad smile lit her face. "Waxahachie!" She punched the air with her fist. "Gotcha!"

She jumped up, grabbed Essie, and danced a little jig as she hugged the sputtering woman. "Hot damn, Essie, she's left a trail! I've got to go tell Dagna."

"You watch your language, Miss Prissy. You're not too big for me to wash your mouth out with soap."

"Yes, ma'am." Susan laughed as she ran from the room.

That night, her face scrubbed clean and her hair caught up in a loose ponytail, Susan sat scrunched in front of her computer. As she scrolled through the pages of the directory on the screen, she absently reached for a cashew nut from the can beside her and popped it into her mouth. Her breath caught as she found the number she sought. Just as she was making a note of the name and address beside it, the doorbell rang.

She decided to ignore it, but the ringing changed to an insistent knocking. Muttering about lousy timing, she rose, tightened the belt on her short silk robe, and hurried to the door. She peered through the peephole and saw Ross standing there, illuminated by the porch light. Shielding her body behind the door, she opened it a crack.

He leaned, stiff-armed, against the jamb, and his red knit shirt stretched tightly across his broad chest. "Evening, ma'am. I was wondering if I could borrow a little sugar."

Amused, she cocked a brow. "I don't see a cup."

A familiar devilish grin spread across his face. "The kind of sugar I have a hankering for doesn't come in a cup." His exaggerated drawl was blatantly suggestive. "Are you going to leave me panting on the porch, or can I come in?"

She laughed nervously. "I'm not dressed."

"Now that sounds mighty interesting."

"I mean I have on my robe."

"Aw, shoot, I thought you meant you were waiting for me in nothing but a smile. But if my seeing you in your robe doesn't bother you, it won't bother me."

She hesitated a moment, then opened the door for him to enter. He sauntered in, and his gaze slowly slid upward from her red-tipped toes over the long expanse of her bare legs and lingered here and there along her body before his eyes met hers. His nostrils flared, and his eyes seemed to pulsate from the depths of their inky darkness. That hungry look paralyzed her lungs, and chill bumps broke out on her skin. He moved closer and took her in his arms.

"I was wrong," he said. "I'm bothered." His lips moved over hers in a testing kiss. "You taste like salt instead of sugar."

"It's from the nuts. Cashews. I was eating cashews."

"I like cashews, too."

His tongue slowly outlined her mouth, licking the traces of salt, then bathing the fullness of her lips with slow savoring strokes. The erotic sensation unfurled an aching deep within her body and turned her legs to useless blobs of protoplasm. She clung to his shoulders for support.

His hands glided over her back, smoothing over the thin silk covering her bare skin. "I tried to call you," he said, his voice thick as he brushed his lips over her temple. "The line was busy."

"I'm using the modem." She was turning to boneless mush against his broad expanse.

"I see. I thought you might like to go out for a pizza or something." His hands continued their lazy circling, slipping lower with each pass. "What are you wearing under this thing?"

"Nothing much."

"Maybe we can send out for pizza." His hands slipped over the curve of her bottom. "Later."

Warning bells went off in Susan's head. "You're going a little too fast for me. I think I'd better get dressed."

He continued to hold her for a moment, then took a deep breath and blew it out in a big whoosh. "Maybe you'd better. Darlin', you can turn me inside out quicker than any other woman I've ever known."

A sudden realization clutched her chest. "And have there been many?"

"Many what?"

"Women."

He smiled in that engaging way of his that crinkled his eyes and deepened the grooves along his cheeks. "Now, Sin, I've never been one to kiss and tell."

She drew herself up to her full height and glared at him. "And I've never been one for recreational sex. I don't plan to be just another notch on some cowboy's bedpost."

She tried to wiggle from his grasp, but he held her firmly. He looked puzzled. "What brought that on?"

A quick answer eluded her. What had brought that on? She'd been as involved as he'd been. She thought for a moment, then answered honestly, "Self-preservation, I suppose. For some reason, you frighten me."

His brows went up. "Me? Why, sugar, I'm just a big old puppy dog. I'd never hurt you."

"But you're so . . . so *male*."

He laughed. "Well, I hope to shout I am. I'd make a funny looking woman." His hand went to the gun clipped to his belt. "Does this bother you?" He touched the star on his shirt. "Or this?"

She shook her head. "No, not really. I'm not sure what it is. It sounds crazy, but you seem kind of . . . overwhelming sometimes. It makes me nervous."

Ross dropped a quick kiss on her forehead. "Don't you worry about it, darlin'. We'll take things slow and easy." He patted her bottom and stepped back. "Grab on a pair of jeans, and we'll go get a bite to eat. Okay?"

Watching her lovely long legs as she retreated into her bedroom, Ross couldn't help but wonder how they would feel wrapped around him. Shaking off the thought that would only make his jeans painfully tighter if he pursued it, he walked over to the aquarium and watched the turtles crawling around on the rock protruding from the water. "I damned near blew it, guys. But I've got an itch for that little lady that's got me hotter than a goat in a pepper patch." He reached out to touch Bond and Moneypenny, but one skittered away and the other drew into its shell.

He shrugged and wandered around the room, pulling out a book here and there to flip through the pages. Restless, he walked over to the computer. What looked like a page from a criss-cross directory was on the screen. He sat down and scrolled the information up until he could see that it was from Waxahachie. He noted a photocopy of Dagna's telephone bill on the desk and the name and address Susan had scribbled on a pad. What was she up to?

"What are you doing?"

He whirled around in the chair at the sound of her voice. "Checking out your computer system. It's a fine one. What's so interesting in Waxahachie?"

"I was looking up the number that Maureen Potts called from Dagna's house. It's probably her daughter, and I thought it might help me locate her."

"Why not just call and see?"

"I did. The phone's been disconnected—she's probably moved—but I plan to go there and question the neighbors."

He caught her hands and pulled her between his spread legs. "Hon, why don't you give this information to Bottoms and let the pros handle it?"

"I gave the phone bill to Leonard this afternoon. He tossed it aside and said it probably wouldn't amount to anything, but he'd try to get around to it in a couple of days." She made a disgusted face. "Good thing I made a copy for myself."

"Let the man do his job. I don't want you to get mixed up in this. We don't know who we're dealing with here. Could be some tough customers. I don't want you hurt." He drew one of her hands to his lips and kissed the back of her wrist.

"I can take care of myself, Mr. Texas Ranger. I've been doing it for a lot of years. In the morning, I'm flying to Dallas, then driving to Waxahachie."

"But, darlin'—"

She bent over and, nose to nose, glared at him. "Watch my lips. I'm going," she enunciated clearly. "Now do you want pizza or not?"

He chuckled and rolled his forehead against hers. "You're getting to be a right feisty little thing, aren't you?"

"You can bet the farm on it, big fella."

A few minutes later, they strolled into the neighborhood pizzeria, the dim, smoky room deliciously scented with Italian spices and crisping crusts. Since it was past the hour for family meals, only a few of the tables, decorated with red-checkered cloths and flickering candles in Chianti bottles, were occupied. Ross steered her toward a booth in an alcove secluded by latticework and plastic grapevines.

As they passed a table of girls with wildly moussed bangs, Susan couldn't help but notice the elbow-poking and eye-rolling directed at Ross. A few giggles and sighs followed in their wake.

With his arm around her waist, he whispered in her ear, "This place okay, hon?"

A tiny, self-satisfied smile stole over her mouth at the knowledge that she was with this gorgeous man, and that he seemed oblivious to anyone but her. She slipped into the booth. "This is fine."

He tossed his hat onto the opposite seat and slid in after it. "And how do you like your pizza, Miss Sin?"

"With anything except onions and anchovies."

"Onions, I can take or leave but, to tell the

truth—" he leaned over and whispered conspiratorially—"I always figured anchovies were for sissies."

"And trying to chew those nasty little things reminds me of trying to eat eyelashes. The only thing worse I can think of is liver." She shuddered.

"I knew you were a lady after my own heart. I hate the stuff. I'd just as soon chew a mouthful of—" He cleared his throat and grinned. " 'Scuse me. I almost repeated what I told my mother once, and I lost my bike for a week. After that, when we had liver, I hid what I could under my peas and put the rest in my pocket to feed to the dog later. I don't think I ever fooled anybody, but Mama never said anything."

She laughed. "I'll bet you were a handful as a child."

"Naw. My brothers and I were just lively. My parents were pretty good sports. You'll like Eleanor."

"Eleanor?"

"My mother. She's a sweetheart. In some ways, you kind of remind me of her."

Susan's heart gave a little leap. In what ways? she wanted to ask. And did he plan on introducing her to his mother? That almost sounded— No, no, she told herself. He was simply making conversation.

The waitress arrived with water, and Ross turned to order. Idly running her finger around the rim of her glass, Susan thought of the normal, happy childhood Ross must have had with two loving parents and siblings to play with. The only stable thing in her youth had been Dagna and books. She didn't feel the pride and affection for her mother that Ross naturally exuded for his.

After the waitress left, Ross captured her hand in his and rubbed his thumb across her knuckles. "What's the matter, darlin'? You seem sad."

She looked up to find genuine concern etched across his face. "No, just thinking," she said, forcing a smile.

"No thinking allowed tonight, Sin. Don't you know that too much thinking will rot your brain cells and make you sterile?"

Laughing, she cocked an eyebrow. "Sterile?"

"That's what I've heard." He tugged her hand and pulled her from the booth. "Come on. Let's go play the video games while we wait."

"But I've never played a video game in my life."

He feigned shock. "Well, sweet Sin, your education is seriously lacking." With his arm around her waist, he hugged her close to his side and headed for the video machines across the room. "Lucky for you, I'm a bona fide expert. I'll teach you all the tricks of the game."

And he tried. But concentration was impossible when he stood so close behind her that she could feel his badge pressed against her shoulder and his belt buckle against the small of her back.

"Now!" he instructed as an alien space ship shot across the screen, but her fingers couldn't function to press the fire buttons when his breath stirred beside her ear and sent shivers rippling over her skin.

"I'm not very good at this, Ross."

His hands resting on the machine in front of her so that she was caught between his big body and the video, he nuzzled her cheek and chuckled. "Who cares? I'd feed the blamed thing quarters all night long just to stand here and snuggle with you. Unfortunately, it looks like our pizza is ready. If you want to keep playing, I'm more than willing to let it sit and order another one later."

The obvious innuendo in his words and the little nip at her earlobe sent a new crop of shivers over her. "Oh, no. I'm starving," she said quickly. *Susan Sinclair, you're such a dull putz,* she thought to herself. Why couldn't she say something suggestive, engage in a bit of sexual banter instead of wanting to bolt like a deer that had smelled a predator?

She didn't know if she was relieved or disappointed when he stepped back. Ross's blatant virility inundated her emotions, emotions she'd held in check for years. The thought of getting truly involved with a man of Ross's caliber scared the pants off her.

Instead of playing the scene coolly, like a blithering idiot she hurried to the booth where the waitress had just placed a pitcher of beer and a giant double-cheese pizza heaped with everything except onions and anchovies. Ross slid in across from her and gave her a smoldering look that could have heated the ovens for a month.

For a moment, she went still. One part of her wanted to hold his stare and give him back a scorching one of her own. But the more familiar part looked away and fumbled for a slice of pizza.

"Smells good. I'm really hungry," she said inanely.

"Me too, Sin, darlin'," he drawled, suggestion slathering his words. "Me too."

Almost able to feel the caress of his eyes and his voice, she snatched up a slice of the steamy concoction and took a big bite.

Hot cheese seared the roof of her mouth. Knowing that Ross was watching her and panicked at her predicament, she opened her lips slightly, tried to jiggle the blistering morsel around with her tongue, and breathe in cool air to quench the fire. It didn't help. Tears came to her eyes.

Ross grabbed a napkin and held it under her chin. "Spit it out!"

She whimpered. For a second she couldn't decide which was worse: total mortification or losing a few layers of skin.

"Spit it out!"

She spit.

He shoved a glass of iced water into her hand and muttered, "Damned fool!"

Past the worst of her shame, Susan gulped the water. "I'm sorry."

"For what?"

"For being such a damned fool."

"Honey, I didn't mean you. I meant that sonofa—that jerk who baked the damned thing too hot. I've a good mind to—" A ferocious scowl on his face, he started to rise.

She waved him back down. "Ross, pizzas are supposed to be baked hot. I shouldn't have bitten into it so quickly." She took another sip of water and rolled an ice cube inside her mouth.

"Are you okay?"

Since he looked as if he'd take on a bear if she said otherwise, she smiled. "I'm fine."

He drew his brows together and studied her intently. "Sure?"

She nodded. Strangely enough, even her embarrassment had vanished. She had the strongest urge to hug him for being so dear about the whole episode.

"Now the secret to eating double-cheese pizza, sweetheart, is to drink some beer first. Numbs the tongue and lays a protective coat over the roof of your mouth."

She fought a smile. "Is that so?"

He gave her a devilish grin. "Now, darlin', would I kid you?"

She hooted with laughter. "In a shot."

"Why, Sin, you've wounded me to the quick."

"I don't think you could be wounded with a buzz saw, Ross Berringer." She gingerly took a bite of food and blotted her lips. "I've been meaning to tell you something. It's sort of a confession."

He waited, brows raised, while she twisted her napkin. "You make it sound serious. You're not wanted for mooning the mayor, are you?"

"*Me?*" She rolled her eyes. "I'm hardly the type. No, it's . . . it's . . . well, nobody really calls me Sin. I made that up."

His face relaxed. "Well, *I'm* going to call you Sin. I like Sin," he drawled. "Except on Sunday." A lopsided grin spread across his mouth as he reached for her hand. His thumb drew lazy circles inside her palm. "And I could forget Sundays with a little encouragement."

Susan went hot all over and pizza had nothing to do with her condition. Sure that her cheeks were blazing with color, she tugged her hand away.

"Now there you go again," he said, "pulling into that shell. Do I embarrass you?"

"Sometimes. Mostly I embarrass myself. I wish I could be as comfortable with myself as you are. Nothing seems to bother you."

"I've never been accused of being shy. And you don't have to be shy around me either. Just loosen up, hon, and let 'er rip. Do what you want to do, and say what you want to say. Life's a helluva lot more fun that way."

They sat in the booth and laughed and talked long after the pizza was gone. When it became evident that they were the last patrons in the place, they reluctantly left.

When Ross walked her to the door of her town house, he kissed her gently. "Mouth still blistered?" When she shook her head, he kissed her again—less gently. His tongue eased over hers to test and explore. "Umm," he murmured. "Feels mighty fine to me. Why don't we continue this inside?"

"I . . . I . . ."

He sighed. "Okay, darlin', I get the message. I'll go to my lonely bed alone. For tonight. I'll see you tomorrow." He kissed the tip of her nose.

"I'm going to Waxahachie, remember?"

"Oh, hell, honey, forget about Waxahachie. You just tend to your bookstore and let the law handle Maureen Potts. Don't fret your pretty little head about it for one minute."

Like salt poured into a wound, his supercilious male attitude sent old pain and fury racing through her. She stiffened her spine and glared at him. "Don't talk to me as if I were a dithering bubblehead. I resent it. I told you that I'm going!"

"You pick the damnedest times to stiffen your back and get feisty. Sin, sugar, it's my nature to want to protect you."

"I don't need protecting, thank you very much. I'm not a helpless, fluttery sort with no more gumption than a bowl of pea soup. If that's the kind of woman your nature calls for, you're barking up the wrong tree with me. I am not now, nor will I ever be, a dependent female who needs a man to think for her."

He grinned and tried to gather her into his arms. "Did I ever tell you that you've got great legs?"

"Stow it, Ranger." She shoved him away, stomped inside, and slammed the door.


Susan shoved her small bag in the overhead compartment, scooted into the window seat, and buckled her belt. She was idly turning the pages of a magazine when a man in a dark suit sat down beside her. She glanced up, then did a double take when she recognized the familiar black hat and the face under it.

"Ross Berringer, what are you doing here?"

"Got a couple of days off, and I thought I'd mosey up to Waxahachie and see the sights."

She glared at him. "I don't think I've ever known anyone who vacationed in Waxahachie. I hope you have fun."

He chuckled and leaned back, resettling his hat over his eyes, stretching out his long legs, and lacing his fingers across his big silver belt buckle. "Think I'll take a snooze. Wake me when the peanuts come. I missed breakfast."

Something about his confident sprawl galled

her. She started to say something nasty, then clamped her lips shut and went back to her magazine, snapping pages furiously and not seeing a word or picture that was printed.

She didn't have to wake him. The flight attendant, a petite blond with deep dimples, put her hand on his shoulder—and it lingered there, Susan thought, a great deal longer than necessary—to get his attention. Eyelashes fluttering like crazy, Tinkerbell served Ross coffee, orange juice, and a half dozen foil packets of peanuts along with fawning smiles. Susan felt lucky to get a half glass of tepid tomato juice.

Once they arrived at the Dallas-Fort Worth airport, Susan tried to ignore Ross and his suit bag. Since he insisted on carrying her overnighter and walking beside her, it was difficult. She headed straight for the car rental phones.

"What are you doing?" Ross asked.

"You don't seem to listen to me. I am renting a car to drive to Waxahachie," she pronounced in a tone usually intended for two-year-olds.

"Why don't you ride with me? I already have a car reserved."

She clenched her teeth. "You're determined to make my life miserable, aren't you?"

He grinned. "Naw, honey. I'm determined to keep your cute little fanny out of trouble." He patted her bottom, took her elbow, and whisked her to the rental agency bus.

She didn't protest too much. For all her bluster, having a man concerned about her well-being was . . . different . . . pleasant. She discovered that she enjoyed being cosseted. Sometimes. Not like her mother, of course, but occasionally was nice.

Usually, she'd been the caretaker. Her ex-husband had been the stereotypical absent-minded professor, so wrapped up in academic thoughts and theories that frequently he'd forgotten that she was around. Once, after a conference in Baton Rouge, he'd driven halfway home before he had remembered that she was standing in front of the hotel, waiting with their bags.

Thomas had been such a dork.

At the rental agency, Ross picked up keys from the desk and steered Susan outside to the lot where their car was waiting. He opened the trunk of a big, black, top-of-the-line luxury car to stow their luggage.

Her eyes widened. "A Cadillac? You've got to be kidding."

He shrugged. "I wanted you to be comfortable."

"But—"

"I've got long legs."

"But—"

He silenced her with a quick kiss. "Humor me, sweetheart."

When they pulled away, Susan said, "I'm going to pay half."

"I can handle it."

"I said I was going to pay half, and I will. I don't know what sort of salary a Texas Ranger makes, but it can't be enough to fritter away on renting Cadillacs with cellular phones."

He laughed. "My mother's going to love you. But relax, babe. The car's not costing me anything."

"Surely you're not expecting the *taxpayers* to pay for such an extravagance!"

"Nope."

She waited for further explanation, but none came. They drove down the expressway for several minutes before Susan's curiosity became an incessant itch. She crossed and uncrossed her legs. She toyed with the gold chain at the throat of her beige silk blouse. She fluffed her hair and smoothed her skirt. Finally, when she could stand it no longer, she asked, "Are you going to tell me or not?"

"Tell you what, honey?"

She rolled her eyes. "Honestly, Ross, for someone who's usually gregarious, you can turn into a clam at the most irritating times. Why don't you have to pay for the car?"

He gave her a lopsided grin. "Nosy little thing aren't you? You remind me of Cory."

"Who's Cory?"

"My brother Holt's wife. He's a Ranger, too, and it took Cory a while to understand that there are lots of things that we can't talk about. 'Secret Ranger business' she calls it."

"Well, I can understand, of course, with investigations and so forth, that some things must be kept confidential, but I can't imagine what that has to do with your not having to pay for this Cadillac. Are you trying to sidetrack me? I should warn you: I'm like a snapping turtle. Once I sink my teeth in something, I don't let go."

"Like Bond or Moneypenny?"

"No, they're red-eared turtles. Are you lying to me about the car from some sense of machismo so I won't insist on paying my share, or are you involved in graft?"

He chuckled. "Neither. Do you mind if we stop

for lunch a little early? Those peanuts aren't holding me. I'm so hungry, my stomach thinks my throat is cut."

She crossed her arms in a huff. "Ross Berringer, sometimes you make me so mad I could spit!"

"Does that mean you don't want to stop?"

"You're driving," she muttered. "And I'm beginning to think I'm going to regret it."

He exited the freeway and pulled into the parking lot of a cafeteria. "The food's good here, and it won't delay us long." When he helped her out of the car, her lips were still pursed in exasperation. He tilted her chin and gave her a hasty peck. "My brother owns the rental agency."

"Oh." She planted her fists on her hips and cocked her head up at him. "Why didn't you simply say so in the first place?"

He grinned and gathered her against his side. "Because I like the way your beautiful eyes shoot sparks when you get riled. Did I ever tell you that your eyes remind me of a distant summer rainstorm?"

She melted. How could she stay angry with someone who said things like that?

"No," Susan said. "Absolutely not. I'm going to talk to the neighbors in the apartment building by myself. Pull up right here and park so you'll be out of sight."

"You're a bossy little thing, aren't you?"

"Yep. Nosy and bossy. If you don't like it, that's tough. You can just tootle back to Beaumont and let me tend to this alone."

He chuckled—Susan could have almost sworn that she heard a hint of patronage in that chuckle—and said, "I think you're cuter than a bug's ear when you get on your high horse, sugar. Not too many people sass me. I guess it's my size."

"And your badge. And your gun. You're intimidating, Ross. By the way, how did you get on the plane with your gun?"

"I had to go through a lot of bureaucratic red tape. That's why I missed breakfast."

"Well, anyway, since you *are* so intimidating, people won't talk as freely to you as they will to me. Especially with my cover."

"Your *cover*?" He looked amused. She wanted to pinch him.

"Certainly, my cover. That's why I wanted to stop at the drugstore." She took a plain white sack from her shoulder bag, shook it out, and transferred the plastic bowls she'd bought into it. She pulled the drawstring with a snap. "Voilà! I'm a Tupperware lady trying to deliver Mary Alice's order to her. Everybody buys Tupperware, and it's logical that I'll need her address to see that she gets it. Isn't it a peachy cover?"

He ran his hand over his mouth and cleared his throat. "Just peachy."

"Are you laughing at me?"

With the side of his index finger, he rubbed the cleft in her chin and smiled warmly. "I wouldn't think of it, darlin'. You go ask your questions."

As Susan strode purposefully away with her sack, Ross laughed and shook his head. She

was something else. When she got the bit between her teeth, there was no stopping her, not
without a fight. And with her, he wanted to be a
lover, not a fighter. He didn't think she could get
into trouble by asking a few questions. If he'd
thought otherwise, he'd have gone with her,
even if it put her nose out of joint. She probably
didn't stand a snowball's chance in hell of finding out anything useful, but if it made her
happy to do some poking around, he'd indulge
her.

He'd planned to go to Waco on his days off and
pack his stuff, but, hell, it could wait. He'd
much rather spend his time with Susan.

While he waited, as a matter of protocol, he
called the Ranger office that covered Ellis
County as well as the headquarters in Dallas to
let them know he was in the area investigating a
case. He asked both offices to check on Mary
Alice Whiteside, giving them her last known
address and telling them he'd check back later.

Courtesies taken care of, he phoned his
brother Paul's office in Dallas. He went through
three secretaries before Paul came on the line.

"Ross," his brother said, "good to hear from
you. Did you get the car okay?"

"Yes, thanks. I'm sitting in it now in beautiful
downtown Waxahachie. Is the hotel set?"

"No problem. But Mama's going to be upset if
she finds out you were in town and didn't see
her."

"Then we won't tell her, will we? I'm with a
lady."

"Aha," Paul said, laughing. "And I'll bet, knowing you, that she's not one you could bring
home to Mama."

Ross felt a prickle of irritation. "She's a very nice lady—and I emphasize *lady,* big brother. Miss Eleanor will love her, and I plan on getting the two of them together. But not this trip."

"So that's the way the wind blows, hmm? It's about time you settled down and left your rowdy ways behind."

"Rowdy? Me?"

Paul laughed again, and they talked a little business before Ross hung up. He checked his watch. Susan had been gone for almost half an hour. He thrummed his fingers on the steering wheel, turned on the radio, then turned it off. He checked his watch again.

What if she *had* run into trouble? He felt a ripple of cold dread skitter up his backbone. Hell, he was going to go see about her. He had the door half open when he saw her coming, head down and shoulders slumped. He went to meet her.

"What took you so long? I was beginning to worry."

"I've been asking questions. The manager said that the police picked up her husband, Rodney Whiteside, about two weeks ago after he and Mary Alice had a loud fight—I think he was abusing her—and last week Mary Alice and her two children left in the middle of the night owing a month's rent. I talked to several of her neighbors. None of them knew much. But one of them invited me in for coffee and booked a Tupperware party."

Ross's shoulders shook with silent laughter.

"It's not funny, Ross. I was counting on information."

He put his arm around her and kissed her

forehead. "I know, honey. I'm sorry. Let's check with the local PD."

As they drove away, Susan said, "Edna—she's the one who booked the party—was very friendly and talkative. She simply didn't know where Mary Alice went. She figured maybe she went back to Dallas to get her old job back in some country and western place she used to—" She stopped abruptly, and Ross could almost see a light bulb flash in her mind. "I've got it. I've got it! I know where we can find her."

# Five

"Slippery Sam's Saloon?" Ross frowned. "How did you come up with that idea?"

Susan dug around in her shoulder bag, pulled out a plastic swizzle stick with a tiny spur on the end, and waved it. "From this. I found it in the garbage. Dagna had never seen it before, so it must have been Maureen's. It seems logical that she might have saved it from where her daughter worked."

"I don't know. Seems kind of farfetched to me."

"Just humor me, okay?"

He chuckled. "You got it."

Their visit to the local police turned up nothing new. Rodney Whiteside was out on bail, and the address listed was the same one they'd checked earlier. They headed back to Dallas to locate Slippery Sam's.

Situated on the north side of the city, the huge saloon resembled a storefront from an old west town. The parking lot, which could have held at least three hundred cars, was empty, and the saloon's doors were locked. They walked around to the back of the barnlike structure and spied a beefy man carrying trash to a dumpster.

"Afternoon." Ross touched the brim of his hat. "We're looking for the manager."

"Ain't here," the man said, scowling. "Ain't nobody here but the cleanup crew. Place don't open till six. Show starts at eight." He tossed the bags he carried into the dumpster.

"Any idea how we might find the manager?"

"Ain't here. Ain't nobody here but the cleanup crew. Place opens at six. Come back then." He walked inside and slammed the door.

"Friendly cuss," Ross commented. "We've got a couple of hours to kill. Why don't we check into a hotel and come back after we have dinner?"

"Oh, dear. I didn't make reservations anywhere. I wasn't sure if I'd be staying overnight. Or where."

"Don't worry. I took care of it."

She gave him a sideways glance as they walked back to the car. "Pretty sure of yourself, weren't you? I hope you reserved two rooms."

"And if I didn't?"

She patted the fender. "Then you can sleep in this nice, comfortable Cadillac."

He caught her neck in the crook of his arm, drew her close and nuzzled her ear. "Aw, Sin, you wouldn't do that to a fellow, would you?"

Chill bumps raced over her skin, and she hesitated a moment, savoring the warmth of his breath and the heady stirring of desire his nearness always bred.

"You and I are going to be so good together,"

he murmured, his tongue tracing the edge of her ear. "So good."

*So good,* her thoughts echoed as her knees began to buckle. *So good.* A car horn tooted and someone yelled something. She jerked away. "I've told you how I feel about being a notch on your bedpost."

"But, honey—"

"Two rooms," she said emphatically. "And I'll pay for mine."

Susan was stunned when the bellboy led them into a lavish suite complete with fresh flowers on the French provincial tables. While Ross tipped the boy, she strolled over to the corner window overlooking the shimmering glass skyline.

Ross wrapped his arms around her waist from behind and rested his chin atop her head. Automatically, she leaned back against his solid frame. "Like it?" he asked. "There are two bedrooms."

"It's beautiful, but it's going to play the very devil with my budget."

"Don't worry about it. It's free."

Her brow cocked, she turned to look at him. "Your brother again?"

He grinned. "Paul sometimes comes in handy."

"Is he married?"

"Divorced."

She wandered around the room and stopped to stroke the silk of a chair back and run her fingers over the fine craftsmanship of the carved cherrywood crest rail. "He must be very rich."

Ross shrugged. "Some might say so. Do rich men turn you on?"

"Heavens, no." She wrinkled her nose and shuddered. "They turn me off. That's my mother's game. Her motto is: It's as easy to fall in love with a rich man as a poor one. She'd never give the time of day to a man whose income was less than six figures. But I prefer plain old meat and potatoes folks myself."

He took off his coat and tossed it on the sofa with his hat. "That's me, babe. I'm a meat and potatoes man all the way." He yanked off his tie and rolled up his sleeves.

"Does it bother you?" she asked.

"Being a meat and potatoes man? Shoot, nothing I like better than a good chicken-fried steak with mashed potatoes and cream gravy."

"No, I meant having a brother who's rich."

"Naw, Paul loves to chase dollars, and Holt and I prefer to chase desperados. Everybody's happy. How about a drink?" He walked over to the bar and examined the stock. "We've got beer, wine, and anything else you could name. How about a martini or a bloody Mary?"

"I'd love a diet cola."

"You got it."

Ross busied himself fixing her cola. He'd nearly stepped in it, he thought. Hell, he'd wanted to impress her with the fancy digs. He should have booked a pair of rooms at the Holiday Inn. How was she going to take it when she found out that the hotel was partly his? Paul owned the car rental agency independently while Ross and Holt had the ranch, but a fourth of nearly everything else the Berringer family owned was his, including several of those buildings that Susan was staring out the window at. And the ranch he and his twin inherited from Grandpa Holt Ross had turned out to have a lake of oil under the pastureland.

He'd better cancel dinner at the Old Warsaw and take her to McDonald's instead. One day soon, when things were more settled between them, he'd find a way to explain the money. He shook his head and laughed to himself. Susan was the first woman he'd ever known who was put off by wealth, which was why he didn't advertise that he was one of the Dallas Berringers. That six figure income Susan's mother was enamored of was a drop in the bucket compared to what he made.

He grabbed her cola and a longneck beer for himself and took them to the coffee table. "All that talk about meat and potatoes made me hungry. You like chicken-fried steak?"

"Love it."

"I know a great place. Why don't we put on our jeans and go eat before we mosey back to Slippery Sam's."

"I didn't bring any jeans, but I have slacks. Will I be out of place?"

"Naw, babe, just be comfortable. I need to make a couple of phone calls and grab a shower."

"Me too."

His eyes took on a naughty gleam. "Wanna share my shower?"

She swatted him playfully. "Don't you ever quit? I meant I need to make some calls too. I have to tell Nadine that I won't be in tomorrow, and I want to check on Dagna."

"Tell Dagna that I wish she was here to go dancing with us."

"But we're not going dancing."

"Babe, Slippery Sam's Saloon is a dance hall. No need to let it go to waste. We'll have a few brews and boogie." He pulled her into his arms and two-stepped her across the room doing an exaggerated wiggle with his bottom and pumping her arm up and down. He stopped abruptly. "You do like to dance, don't you?"

"I love to dance."

He grinned. "See, I knew you were a gal after my own heart."

He bent down to kiss her. He meant for it to be a quick peck, but the softness of her lips enticed him to linger. Her taste and her sweet smell were an aphrodisiac he couldn't resist. He deepened the kiss and pulled her closer to mold her soft curves against him.

Oh, Lord, he was falling. Falling hard.

Oh, Lord, she was falling. Falling hard. Trying to push the thought from her mind, she gave her hair a few vigorous swipes, then tossed her brush back in her shoulder bag. In the mirror of the ladies' room where they'd had dinner, she retouched her lipstick and straightened the blue sweater she wore.

She couldn't allow herself to get emotionally entangled with a man like Ross. Oh, sure, he was exciting and fun and the sexiest man she'd ever met. He was tender and sweet and outrageous. He made her laugh, and he made her body quiver like gelatin in an earthquake when he kissed her.

But sometimes he also made her want to snuggle up against his broad chest and let him take care of things. That scared her. Ross was an authoritative, masterful person—such behavior was as natural for him as breathing—but she'd struggled all her life to be emotionally independent. She wouldn't allow herself to be controlled by anyone or become so wrapped up in any man that she couldn't function without him. Intimacy at the cost of her identity was too high a price to pay. She might eventually take Ross into her bed, but she darned sure wasn't going to let him mess with her heart. Falling head over heels in love was a certain road to grief.

Resolve stiffened, she went to meet Ross.

It was after seven when they arrived at Slippery Sam's, and the parking lot was filling up fast. Inside the darkened dance hall, neon signs flashed competing beer advertisements from every wall, and a foot-stomping Hank Williams, Jr., song vibrated the wooden floor and jiggled the assortment of giant John Wayne photographs, singletrees, and spurs nailed here and there along with other western memorabilia.

The air, stirred by a dozen fans attached to the rough-beamed ceiling, smelled of cigarettes and an anonymous amalgam of fried food. A hovering atmosphere of barely leashed wildness permeated the place. Susan never frequented such spots, and she was glad to have the comfort of Ross's hand at her waist.

"Howdy, pardner," said one of a pair of smiling cowboys, who looked more like students from the local university's drama department than ranch hands. "Welcome to Slippery Sam's Saloon."

"Evenin'," Ross said, touching the brim of his black hat.

"We're proud to have ya drop by. Come on in and stay a spell," said the other. "Tonight, we've got Hoot Henry and the Hell-raisers. Live. Wipe your boots, check your pistol here, and have a good time. That'll be ten dollars cover charge."

Ross peeled a bill from his money clip and said, "I think I'll keep my pistol. Never can tell when I might run into a gunslinger out to make a name for himself."

The young men laughed. "Are you jivin' us, man?" one asked.

Ross flipped open his jean jacket to reveal the star pinned to his shirt. Both cowboys sobered. Susan pressed her lips together to keep from laughing at the expressions that passed between the two greeters.

"Where can we find the manager?" Ross asked.

"He's not here. Honest. Nita, the assistant manager, is around somewhere. I'll find her for you. If you want to wait in the bar, it's quieter there."

Ross steered Susan to the bar, and they took stools a few seats away from a quartet of motley urban cowboys who were drinking beer. The thick-necked one, who wore a plaid shirt stretched over his pot belly, eyed her and said something to his buddies. They ogled her, then laughed.

Susan shivered and turned away quickly. "Nice clientele."

"You want to leave, hon?"

"No, certainly not. But they give me the creeps."

"Ignore them. They've got no manners, but they're just good old boys out to have a little fun."

"What'll it be, folks?" the bartender asked.

Susan wiggled on the bar stool and thought for a minute. "I'll have a banana daiquiri."

Ross ordered a beer. "Real two-fisted drinker aren't you, babe?" he commented, looking amused.

"Liquor makes me do strange things. Two drinks and my nose goes numb. Three, and I become totally uninhibited."

With a lascivious grin, he said, "I'll have to remember to ply you with drinks."

She shook her head. "Oh, no, you won't. After I made a fool of myself a few times, I've learned to stop at the numb nose stage."

Their drinks were served and they had a few sips before a redhead in skin-tight jeans sidled up to the bar and smiled at Ross.

"I'm Nita Fisher, the assistant manager," she said. "May I help you?"

Ross flashed his I.D., then said, "We're trying to locate a Mary Alice Whiteside who may have worked here."

"The name isn't familiar," the redhead said, "but I've only been here about three months. You'll need to talk to Sam, the owner, but tonight is his kid's bar mitzvah, and he won't be in until later."

"You mean there really is a Slippery Sam?" Susan asked.

Nita laughed. "There really is. Why don't you two enjoy yourselves, and I'll let you know when Sam comes in."

When she left, Susan asked, "Do you think

we're wasting our time on a wild goose chase?"

"Babe, wild goose chases are a real part of investigations. We may find out something and we may not, but we're not wasting our time. Let's dance." He pulled her to her feet and led her into the main room, zigzagging around tables to the floor.

As Garth Brooks sang a romantic ballad, Ross took her in his arms, holding her close against him so that her head was tucked under his chin. They fit together and moved together perfectly. Ross led with not only the pressure of his hands to guide her but also with subtle, sensuous movements of his entire body.

His arms circled her waist; her hands lay on his upper chest so that her fingertips reached his shoulders. Eyes closed, she rubbed her cheek against the rough denim of his jean jacket and breathed in his scent.

She sighed, snuggled closer, and felt the tempo of his heart increase. Feminine satisfaction made her smile.

The ballad segued into a slow waltz. Wordlessly, his hand sought hers, and their steps changed to the broad, graceful movements of the three-four time. Dancing with him was like gliding on ice. If she'd been wearing a gown and a tiara, she'd have felt like a princess at a formal ball with flickering candles instead of neon beer signs.

When the song ended, they went back to the bar and finished their drinks, ordered fresh ones, and danced some more. Ross told outrageous stories; they laughed and talked, and he scratched her nose when it began to get numb.

Hoot Henry and the Hell-raisers came on and

cut down on a hot rock-a-billy number that had the whole place whistling and clapping.

With his hands at her waist, Ross slid her off the bar stool. Moving to the rhythm, he swiveled his bottom, shook his shoulders, and bumped his hip against hers. "Come on, sugar, let's boogie and get *mean.*"

On the dance floor, they moved apart except for their gazes. His whole body began to stir into a loose limbed series of gyrations that was totally unselfconscious. He drew close, then retreated, teasing her with winks and smiles that matched his exuberance. Her movements, inhibited at first, soon relaxed and she began teasing him as well. With shoulders swiveling and pelvises bumping and grinding, each trying to outdo the other, their dance became seduction in motion. Ross became Male in a primal fertility rite; Susan became Female.

His eyes, heavy lidded and sin black, mesmerized her; his big body taunted her. Fire sparked and flashed between them. Perspiration dampened her face as her pulse quickened and her breathing became rapid and shallow.

When the song ended, Ross drew her against his side and his hand slid down to stroke her hip. "Sweet Sin, you're something else. You make me wish we were back at the hotel alone. I'd like to—" He whispered in her ear activities she'd never considered in her wildest fantasies.

Her eyes widened. She sucked in a startled breath and went warm all over. "I need another drink." She practically ran back to the bar stool and ordered a third banana daiquiri. Or was it her fourth? Who cared? When it came, she gulped it down and fanned herself furiously with the cocktail napkin.

Ross leaned against the bar with one foot on the rail and looked amused. "Warm?"

"The air conditioner must be on the fritz." Before he could comment on her lame excuse, she stood and grabbed her purse. "I have to go to the ladies' room."

She hurried toward the door marked "Mares," ignoring suggestive remarks from the red-neck quartet as she passed by.

Feeling woozy, she splashed cold water on her face, and while she blotted it dry, she leaned against the counter and stared at her reflection. "Mirror, mirror on the wall, who is headed for a fall?"

She leaned closer. "You are, stupid. You're acting crazy! Keep this thing in perspective. You're here to get a lead on Mary Alice and her thieving mother, not to have a hot affair with a Texas Ranger every woman in the place is panting for. He is trouble. Do you hear that? *Trouble.*"

There was a flush from one of the stalls, and a blond cowgirl came out. When she saw that Susan was alone, she cut her eyes to the door, back to Susan, then eased out without washing her hands.

Susan giggled. "See, I told you. Crazy." She wiggled her nose and rubbed it. "Deader than a doorknob." She giggled again. "Oh, well, what the heck."

A few minutes later she sauntered from the ladies' room, swinging her shoulder bag and humming "Tiptoe Through the Tulips."

A thick hand grabbed her wrist. She looked

down at the hairy knuckles, then up at the burly cowboy in the plaid shirt who stood grinning at her. He had a gap between his front teeth and a lecherous gleam in his eyes.

"Let's you and me dance, sweet thang," he said.

She gave him her haughtiest look. "Let's not." She tried to pull her wrist from his grip but she couldn't budge it. "Let me go. You're drunk."

He smirked at his comrades who laughed and egged him on with "Git her, Charlie."

"I seen you rubbin' it all over that other feller, hot britches," Charlie said. "I'd like to get me a little of that myself." His hand still clamped around her wrist, he headed for the dance floor.

Susan dug in her heels and whopped him with her purse. "Let me go, you baboon!"

She might as well have been talking to an octopus. He kept heading toward the floor, dragging her behind him. She grabbed one of the posts that separated the bar from the rest of the room and wrapped one leg around it.

"Let the lady go, buddy," a deep voice commanded. "She's with me."

Susan breathed a sigh of relief when she saw all six feet six of Ross standing there, feet spread apart, black eyes narrowed, and the muscles in his jaw twitching like a flamenco dancer.

"Not anymore, she ain't," Charlie snarled.

"She's mine," Ross said. "I'm telling you one more time to let her go."

Charlie spit out a terse two-word gutter phrase. Ross grabbed the front of Charlie's shirt, gave a short chop to his forearm that uncurled his fingers from Susan's wrist, then flung the drunken cowboy against the bar.

Charlie let out a roar and, fist cocked, ran at Ross. Ross ducked, seized a fistful of plaid collar and butted Charlie's head against the thick cedar post. The man crumpled like a puppet with its strings cut.

"Look out, Ross!" Susan yelled as Charlie's three buddies jumped up and advanced on him.

Ross met a fist as he turned. Two of the cowboys grabbed his arms and the third hit him in the middle. Ross shook off one and clipped his assailant with a quick punch before the pair could get hold of him again.

Susan snatched up a beer bottle and conked one on the head, stunning him momentarily. He shook his head, shoved her aside, and waded back into the three against one melee. Yelling, "Stop, stop!" she jumped on the back of the one holding Ross's right arm. Clinging to him like a monkey, she got a stranglehold around his throat and beat his head with her purse.

Cursing, the man tried to shake her loose, but she held on like a cocklebur.

More people poured into the bar, but Susan was too busy with her opponent to pay much attention. She had him on his knees. A strong arm clamped around her waist and peeled her off the man trying to protect his head from the wicked blows of her purse.

"Ease up, darlin', the bouncers will take care of him," a familiar voice said in her ear.

She jumped up and fell into Ross's arms. "Oh, Ross, I thought they were going to kill you. Why didn't you tell them you were a Texas Ranger?"

He chuckled as he held her close. "I didn't get a chance. Besides, four men against one Ranger is nothing. Haven't you ever heard that it only takes one Ranger to handle a riot?"

She drew back and looked askance. "It was just three men. Don't forget I was handling one of them."

He laughed and hugged her. "And did a damned fine job of it, too. But don't ever do a fool thing like that again. You could have been hurt." He hugged her tighter.

"But I wasn't," she mumbled against his shirt front. "I was trying to free your gun arm."

"Honey, I don't draw my gun unless I have no other choice."

"But—" She pulled back and looked up at him. "Ross! Your poor face. You're bleeding." She touched a spot on his cheekbone. "I'm taking you to the emergency room right now."

"Aw, babe, it's just a scratch."

"Men! It's not a scratch. You'll probably need stitches."

"Don't you want to hear what Sam has to say first?"

"He's here?"

He nodded. "Came in while you were in the bathroom. He's waiting for us in his office."

# Six

With Susan protesting that he needed medical attention first, Ross steered her toward Sam Friedman's office. "Hell, sugar, it's nothing. I've had worse scratches picking blackberries when I was a kid."

"It's *not* a scratch, Ross. A doctor needs to look at it. You're going to have a scar."

"Thanks for worrying about me, darlin', but we need to talk to this guy now. We'll worry about my scar later. Anyway," he said, wiggling one eyebrow and rubbing his hip against her, "I've heard that ladies sometimes think a scar or two is kind of sexy." His mouth curled into a roguish, lopsided grin. "Maybe you'll think I'm ir-re-sistible."

Susan rolled her eyes. "Oh, good grief. Come on, Mr. Macho, and let's get this over with."

When they entered the paneled and plushly carpeted office, the owner stood. Half a head shorter than Susan, Sam Friedman had a heavy jaw and a long upper lip bisected by a thin, black mustache that looked as if it had been painted on with a laundry pen. Ross showed his Ranger I.D. to the wiry man who wore a yellow rose in the lapel of his Mississippi gambler's frock coat.

Ross introduced Susan, and after they were seated, he said, "Mr. Friedman, we're trying to locate a woman named Mary Alice Whiteside. Our information suggests that she may have worked here as a cocktail waitress at one time. Is that true?"

Sam pursed his lips and gingerly ran a hand over his slicked-back hair. "Might be. Why do you ask? Has she done something wrong?"

"Not as far as we know. We just need to ask her a few questions about a case we're working on."

"And what case is that?" Sam asked superciliously.

"I'd rather not say," Ross answered, irritated with the man's evasion. "Did she work here?"

"Yes, but she left about three or four months ago." He pulled a fat cigar from a humidor on his desk and took his time lighting it. "Went to Waxahachie, I believe."

"She's moved from there," Ross said. "Do you have any knowledge of her current whereabouts?"

Friedman rocked back in his plump leather chair, blew out a plume of smoke, then steepled the fingers unoccupied with his expensive cigar in front of his chest. His lips curved into an oily smile. "I'd rather not say."

*Oh, hell*, Ross thought. He hated to deal with these runts with a Napoleon complex who were always trying to prove something. Rearing back in his seat, Ross propped the ankle of one size thirteen boot on the opposite knee, and pushed his hat back. Casually, he brushed open his jacket and rested his hand on the handle of his Berretta. "Rather not . . . or refuse?"

Friedman took another long drag from his cigar and aimed the exhaled smoke toward the ceiling.

"I can't believe this!" Susan, who'd been sitting quietly during the exchange between the two men, jumped to her feet and leaned across the desk, glaring at the cocky little banty rooster. "Listen, Slippery Sam, if you know where she is, you'd better spit it out. We're in a hurry to get to the emergency room. Do you see his injury?" She pointed to the cut on Ross's cheekbone. "The injury he sustained when he was attacked by your drunken patrons while trying to protect me from their lewd advances. You will, of course, pay his medical expenses, and I wouldn't be surprised if there was a lawsuit here. Maybe two. His *and* mine. I'm not accustomed to being accosted by rowdies who have drunk well past their legal consumption limit."

Susan's eyes flashed, and she waved her arms like an avenging angel. Friedman looked as if somebody had goosed him with a cattle prod, and Ross clenched his teeth to keep from laughing.

"Now, now. I don't think there's any call for a lawsuit, Miss Sinclair. Sergeant, send all the medical bills to me, of course. I'll take care of them personally. And you both have my profound apologies for the unfortunate incident. My staff will be given explicit orders never to allow those men back in the saloon. As for the matter of Mary Alice, you'll be pleased to know that I received a telephone inquiry only day before yesterday for a reference. I believe I have the note here." He searched through a stack of papers. "Yes, yes, here it is." He named one of the big casino hotels in Reno, Nevada. "She was a good worker, and I gave her an excellent reference."

Susan hiked up her chin and looked down her nose at Friedman, who had suddenly turned as friendly as a heifer at dinnertime. "Thank you very much. Now if you'll excuse us, we have to get to the hospital." She turned her attention from Slippery Sam. "Ross?"

Biting back a chuckle, he dropped his feet to the floor. "Yes, ma'am. I'm right behind you."

She didn't say another word until they were in the car.

She pulled a wad of tissue from her purse and blotted his cheek. "I can't believe you two sat there posturing like children while you're bleeding. Where is the closest emergency room?"

"Aw, hon, a dab of peroxide and a Band-Aid will fix me up."

Two hours later, when Ross came out of the treatment room with three stitches and a bottle of pain pills, Susan gave him a smug, I-told-you-so little smile.


"You've had a trauma to your body and you need to rest," she said as she led him to the door of his bedroom.

His forearms on her shoulders, he leaned down and kissed each of her eyelids. "But I'll rest much better knowing you're beside me.

What if I should need something during the night?"

Susan looked up at him. "There's a telephone at your fingertips. It's only a tiny cut, Ross. Don't be such a baby."

"How quickly they forget," he said dramatically to an imaginary audience. "A man risks life and limb defending the honor of his lady, and she tosses him aside like an old sack."

She rolled her eyes. "Go to bed, Ross." She gave him a quick peck.

"Yes, ma'am." He returned her kiss, but his lingered to nip and taste and nuzzle.

She pulled away. "Good night, Ross."

"Don't you want to talk about finding Mary Alice?"

"It's late. We'll talk in the morning."

She shoved him through the door and went to her own bedroom. Exhausted after all the hullabaloo of the day, she figured that she'd drop off to sleep the moment she was snuggled between the covers, but it didn't work that way. Going over in her mind the new information about Maureen's daughter, she tossed and turned in bed. Something nagged at her.

The message from Dagna. Sally Innis, who worked in the business office of the telephone company in Vendor, had dropped off a list of long-distance calls made from Dagna's phone since the last billing.

She got out of bed and located the pad where she'd hurriedly taken notes as she'd talked to her grandmother earlier. There were four calls that Dagna didn't recognize. Three, two of them to the same number, had 409 area codes—

which covered southeast Texas—and one had a 702 code.

Susan grabbed the phone directory and flipped through the front pages. There it was. A smug grin spread across her face. Seven oh two. Nevada.

She glanced at her watch. If it was two-thirty in the morning in Texas, it would be twelve-thirty in Nevada. She pondered a moment, then thought, *Why not?* She snatched up the receiver and used her credit card number to dial. Breath held, she listened as the phone rang once, twice.

"Desert Rose Motel," a bored, nasal voice answered.

Heart pounding, Susan said, "Mary Alice Whiteside, please."

"Nobody here by that name."

Her shoulders slumped. "I know she was there a few days ago, and I have to find her. Mary Alice Whiteside. A young woman with two children."

"Sorry, she must have checked out," the nasal voice said.

"Do you know when?"

"You'll have to discuss that with the manager."

"And where is the manager?"

"At this time of night, I imagine he's asleep in bed, honey, where I'd be if I had a lick of sense and a better job."

Susan thanked her and was about to hang up when another question popped into her head. "Wait, wait. What town are you in?"

"Reno, Nevada."

Susan hung up and sat tapping the receiver with her fingernail and staring at the other numbers on the pad. Dare she? She wished fervently for her computer and modem.

The numbers seemed to mock her, tantalize her. What the heck! She dialed the first number and listened to twenty rings before she tried the second. No answer.

"Doodle!" Frustrated, she went to bed and tried to go to sleep. Her mind flitted around like a roadrunner. Why hadn't she brought a book to read? She never went anywhere without a book.

Maybe she'd better check on Ross. She tiptoed through the parlor that separated their rooms— though why she tiptoed when she was barefoot and walking on carpet two inches thick she didn't know—and peered into his room. The glow from city lights coming through the open draperies dimly illuminated the king-size bed. She crept closer.

His eyes were closed, and his deep, measured breath indicated that he was asleep. He lay on his back with arms outflung and legs spread. A sheet covered one leg and veiled the strategic part of his lower body like a modesty drape in an Italian sculpture. The rest of him was bare, including a lean hip the corner of the sheet didn't quite cover.

She stood looking at him for a long time, drawn by some invisible magnet. The man was gorgeous. Beautiful. From his tousled black hair, curling as he slept, to his feet, he was undoubtedly the most handsome man she'd ever encountered. Even his toes were perfect. Again, she was reminded of a classic statue where the second toe was always longer than the big toe, as his were. The curve of his ankle and calf and thigh spoke of strength, yet there was an inherent grace to the contour.

Her fingers itched to slide over his chest with its downy patch of dark hair that trailed down to his navel, then burgeoned briefly again before the sheet obstructed her view. Engrossed in the marvel of his body, she wondered if the concealed parts were as magnificent. She reached out to lift the cover, then jerked her hand back.

*That's perverse*, she told herself. *Voyeuristic.* Still, she lingered, perusing him, trying to find some flaw where there was none. He was fantastically appealing, stunningly . . . *male.*

The sheet stirred. She sucked in a startled breath; her eyes widened and flew to his. His were open, and his white teeth flashed in a huge grin.

She wanted to die.

"You're awake," she said.

"Mmm."

"How . . . long?"

He chuckled. "How . . . long . . . what?"

She felt heat blossom over her face. "How long have you been awake?"

"Since I smelled you come in the room."

"I—I was just checking to see if you were okay. Your . . . injury . . ."

He chuckled again and tapped his cheek. "Love, my injury is here."

"Are you feeling okay?"

"Hell, no. I feel like I'm on fire."

She tested his forehead with her palm. "I don't think you have a fever."

"That's not where the heat is. Come here."

He reached for her, but she backed away. It would be so easy. So easy. But if she ever gave in to the potent emotions swirling and sizzling inside her, she'd be lost. Sucked in, devoured, and lost. Turning, she ran from the room.

Freshly showered, shaved, and dressed, Ross sat beside Susan's bed, drinking his third cup of coffee and watching her sleep. She was curled up on her side with one hand beneath her cheek and the covers under her chin. It was a pity he didn't have X-ray vision. But his imagination had been going crazy for the past ten minutes.

Her mouth was open slightly in a sweet kissable invitation, and her eyes darted back and forth under closed lids. He hoped she was dreaming about him. God knows, he'd spent a few restless nights dreaming about her.

For the first time he really understood why Holt had acted like such a besotted fool over Cory. He felt the same way about Susan. There was only one explanation: he was in love. Had to be. What else could explain the knots in his gut, the feeling of walking on air one minute and being as nervous as a calf at branding time the next? Sometimes he thought his chest was going to bust wide open when he looked at her or held her. And another part of him felt as if it was going to bust, too.

Holy hell, he wanted her. He wanted to shuck his clothes, leap in that bed with her, and love her until her toes curled.

But she was as skittish as those turtles of hers. If she knew what was on his mind right now, she'd probably jump up and start spouting all that crap about not wanting to be another notch on his bedpost. Hell, he wasn't that kind of guy. Sure, he'd had his share of women since he was sixteen, but he wasn't the rutting stud she made him out to be—at least not in the last few years. He'd had a couple of long-term relationships, but no other woman had *ever* made him feel as he felt about Susan. He could barely keep his hands off her, and his heart was long gone.

The sight of her hair fanned across her pillow in sweet, sexy disarray drew his hand. Very carefully, he coiled one light curl around his finger and rubbed it with his thumb. Soft as corn silk.

As he leaned over her, her special scent of peach blossoms and spice wafted up to him. He closed his eyes, clenched his teeth, and shuddered with deep, potent hunger.

Her eyes opened, then widened. "What are you doing here?"

"Watching you sleep. I figured turn about was fair play." Her cheeks flushed, and it tickled him.

"I was checking your injury," she said huffily. "I wasn't acting the voyeur."

He fought a smile. "If you say so. Want some coffee?"

"Please."

He offered her the cup he held. Clutching the sheet to her chest with one hand, she sat up and took the coffee. He could see the pink straps of an undershirt and remembered the sexy little bit of nothing she'd had on the first time he saw her. The memory tightened his britches even more.

She took a sip, then made a face. "It's lukewarm." She set the cup on the nightstand, stretched, and yawned. "What time is it?"

"A little after nine."

"Oh, my goodness, why didn't you wake me earlier?"

"Because you were tired and you looked so cute sleeping that I didn't have the heart. Room service should be here with our breakfast in a minute."

"I'd better get dressed."

"Mmm."

"Ross, you have to leave so I can get up."

"Why? Babe, I've seen you in your skivvies before."

Her eyes narrowed and her mouth puckered up as if she'd bitten into a pickle with too much alum. "You said you turned your head."

He grinned. "I lied."

"Darn your hide, Ross Berringer!" She snatched up a pillow and whacked him over the head.

Laughing, Ross warded off her blows with his arm, then grabbed her wrist and disarmed her. "I'm glad you didn't have your purse handy, sweetheart. I'd have a concussion to go with my cut."

Her fury faded, and she looked horrified. "Oh, Ross, I forgot about your stitches. Did I hurt you?"

He kissed her nose. "No, honey, you didn't hurt me. I was only teasing. I think I hear the door. Want breakfast in bed?"

She shook her head. "I'll put on a robe and be right out."

A few minutes later, after her first cup of hot coffee, she related the new information about

Mary Alice. "So it looks like she's definitely left the state and is in Nevada. I wish I could fly out there and question her."

"Let's do it."

"But I have a business to run, and you have your work to think of as well."

He shrugged. "I had a couple of days off coming, and tomorrow is Saturday."

"Ross, I can't afford to fly all over the country chasing down leads. And neither can you. Nevada is out of your jurisdiction."

"Don't worry about it, babe. I have lots of frequent flyer miles accumulated. It won't cost us a thing to fly there. Finish your breakfast, and while you get dressed, I'll make all the arrangements."

"But—"

Incredulous, Susan's gaze scrutinized the posh interior of the private jet. "You've got to be kidding."

Looking enormously pleased with himself, Ross shrugged. "I have *lots* of frequent flyer miles."

She cocked a skeptical brow.

Laughing, he stretched out in an oversized recliner and pulled her into his lap. "Not buying frequent flyer miles?"

"Not for a single second."

"Well, babe, all the regular flights out today were booked. Besides"—he patted his gun—"I couldn't take my friend here without a ton of red tape I didn't have a couple of hours to deal with."

"You could leave it here, you know."

"Nope. Where I go, it goes. You never can tell

when you might meet up with a rattlesnake," he said, not cracking a smile although devilment danced in his eyes.

Try as she might, she couldn't help but laugh at his outrageous comment. "Aren't you ever serious?"

"Oh, I like to cut up, but when the time comes to get serious, I get serious." With his thumb, he rubbed the indentation in her chin. "I'm serious about you."

Her heart did a quick thrum, and she tried to rise from his lap, but his arms locked around her waist. Attempting to act nonchalant, she held her emotions in check and glanced away to scan the cabin. "Does this plane belong to your brother?"

Ross shrugged. "He owes me a couple of favors." He tossed his hat aside and kissed the corner of her mouth. "Now tell the truth, isn't this more comfortable than being scrunched up in coach?"

Grudgingly, she had to admit that it was. She'd never been in a private jet in her life. And, compared to the commercial planes she traveled, this one was luxurious. After they were in the air, she insisted that Ross take her on a tour—as much to escape sitting in his lap as from curiosity about their classy mode of transportation. Besides the comfortable places for twelve or so, it sported a galley and two large lavatories.

"A *bedroom?*" she said when he opened a door in the rear.

"Sure." He grinned, hooked his arm around her neck, and nuzzled her ear. "Want to join the mile-high club?"

"Ross Berringer! Don't you ever have anything else on your mind?"

He sighed and let her go. "Lately, darlin', I've been fighting a losing battle."

She knew the feeling. She'd told herself constantly that she was a first-class dodo for allowing herself to become more and more involved with Ross. Intellectually, she understood the danger, but her body and her emotions constantly rebelled and scampered after him like lemmings in a kamikaze plunge over a cliff.

They helped themselves to drinks and sat on one of the two plush couches in the cabin. With Susan wielding the pencil, they decided to work the crossword puzzle in the *Dallas Morning News*. But her mind didn't seem to function as well as usual. It was hard to concentrate with him sitting thigh to thigh with her, blowing in her ear, and murmuring how each of her attributes turned him on.

"What's a six letter word for ripe?" she asked, wiggling as his tongue traced the shell of her ear.

"Breast?"

"Ross! Pay attention."

"I'm not attentive?"

"To the puzzle," she said. "What's a five letter word for vocalist?"

"Randy."

"Ross! Get serious."

"Honey, I am serious. Randy Travis. He's a country singer." He nibbled at her earlobe.

When the tip of his tongue ventured down her neck and his hand slid up from her calf to her knee, the lead of her pencil snapped against the paper. Her eyes closed as she drank in the delicious sensations of his stroking. He swallowed her whimper as his lips closed over hers.

The pencil fell from her fingers, and her arms went around him to pull him closer. She ached all over for his touch. Her breasts felt full and needful of his stroking. His hand seemed to sense her silent wishes as it slipped over the curve of her hip to find the swell of her breast and cup it.

She cursed the fabric of her blouse, and his fingers unbuttoned the closure, slowly, maddeningly. The silk slithered off her shoulders as his kiss deepened with a low growl.

He peeled down her camisole, deftly unhooked her bra and pushed it aside. Then he drew back. Automatically, she crossed her arms to cover herself, but he captured her wrists and pulled them apart.

"No, love," he said, his voice a husky whisper. "Let me look. Let me see." His finger circled one taut nipple, then the other. His hand cupped the underside, and he gazed up at her with those black, burning eyes. "Beautiful. So beautiful." He bent and, with his tongue, traced the circles his finger had made.

His lips closed over the tip and gently suckled. Sensation rippled through her breasts and went on and on and on in ever widening rings until it generated a humming, throbbing ache low and deep in her body. She arched her back and dug her fingers into his forearms. She was lost in a haze of desire like nothing she'd ever experienced.

"We'll be landing in Reno in fifteen minutes, Mr. Berringer," a voice said over the intercom.

The pilot's announcement shot through the

haze like a dash of icy water. Horrified by her behavior, Susan pushed Ross away and struggled to cover herself with the camisole.

"Oh, my Lord, Ross, we nearly—I nearly—"

He grinned. "Yeah, I know."

She grabbed her blouse and held it in front of her. "Ross, the pilot's right there, through that little door. I can't believe this."

"Babe, you don't have to worry about Harvey. He knows better than to come in here without being invited."

She stiffened. "I suppose this sort of conduct is old hat to you, but I don't *do* things like this. I've told you before, I won't—"

"—be another notch on my bedpost," he finished for her, scowling as he mimicked the words. "Hell, Sin, you're driving me crazy. I don't usually *do* things like this either. But, sweetheart, I want you so bad that I stay harder than a shotgun barrel."

She pursed her lips and gathered her clothes around her. "Excuse me, I have to make myself presentable."

Snagging her purse on the run, she escaped to the lavatory. When she saw herself in the mirror, she groaned. She closed her eyes and let her hand trail to her breast. It was still wet. She groaned again. How was she ever going to hold out against this man? She'd been a fool to agree to this trip with him. Already she could feel herself slipping into a deep abyss.

# Seven

From a dozen directions in the enormous room, lights flashed, bells rang, and machines spit out coins in a staccato clink of metal against metal. Even in the early afternoon, scores of people—many of them white-haired senior citizens in polyester outfits—sat in front of chrome-colored machines decorated with various combinations of fruit, numbers, and other symbols. Beside them were cardboard cups or buckets full of nickels or dimes or quarters that they fed into the hungry slots with the familiar precision of assembly line workers. In other areas, several intrepid souls clutched racks of silver dollars, which they disposed of with similar rote actions. Only a few players stood around various gaming tables.

Susan tried not to gape as she trailed behind Ross to the reservation desk, but she'd never seen anything like it. She'd never been to Reno or Las Vegas or Atlantic City, Thomas had always preferred to spend vacations in archaeologically significant places. Of course she'd seen gambling casinos in movies and on TV, but the screen hadn't captured the true ambiance of the real thing. Here there was an excitement, an electricity zipping around the room.

Nearby, a red-haired matron in an aqua sweat suit let out a piercing scream as the machine she was playing went berserk with ringing bells and flashing lights. Coins spewed into the trough like a silver waterfall.

"Looks like she hit a jackpot," Ross said.

"It's amazing. She must have won hundreds of dollars worth of coins."

Looking amused, he asked, "Are you getting gambling fever?"

She shook her head. "I'm not much of a gambler. I work too hard for my money to toss it away on a whim. Not everybody here is a success story."

"The secret is to allot only what you can afford to lose and think of it as entertainment."

Ross turned to give his name to the clerk. Susan had insisted that they reserve two simple rooms, and she would pay for her own, thank you very much.

"Ah, Mr. Berringer, welcome. We've been expecting you. Just a moment, please. Mr. Green wanted to be informed of your arrival." The clerk disappeared through a door behind the desk.

"Who's Mr. Green?" Susan asked.

Before Ross had time to answer, a man in a navy blazer came charging out to greet them. The fellow was handsome in a slick, Hollywood way. Tanned and fit, his hair blown dry into a perfect, thick helmet, he smiled broadly, exposing a row of teeth that must have provided a college education for his dentist's kid.

He pumped Ross's hand and slapped him on the back. "How are you doing, big fella? It's good to see you. You haven't been here since you cleaned us out in the poker tournament two years ago. Sorry I was out when you called this morning." Still smiling broadly, he turned to Susan. "And who is this lovely lady?"

Ross introduced Susan to Marty Green, the manager of the hotel. "We're trying to locate a woman who applied for a job here a few days ago. Mary Alice Whiteside. Think you could come up with an address for us?"

"No problem, friend. I'll have my secretary get right on it. In the meantime, go upstairs to your rooms and get settled." Marty snapped his fingers at the clerk. "John, see that Mr. Berringer and his guest are shown to the Belle Starr Suite on seven, compliments of the house."

Susan frowned. Compliments of the house? Why? Too polite to question Ross with others present, she vowed to ask about their special treatment when they were alone.

On their way to the elevators, they passed several boutiques with absolutely heavenly things displayed in the windows. Susan gazed longingly at a blue dress alive with crystals and beads. Fat chance, she thought, allowing herself one last wistful glance.

Ross, who had lagged behind the bellman as she window shopped, said, "Like that dress?"

"It's magnificent."

"Why don't we buy it?"

"You've got to be kidding. It's bound to cost an arm and a leg. Besides, where would I wear it?"

"We can go someplace fancy for dinner to-night."

She looked down at her rumpled silk blouse. "Then I may buy another top of some kind. My travel wardrobe is sadly limited. I didn't intend to be gone this long, and I didn't pack enough clothes."

He hooked his arm around her neck and pecked her cheek. "Darlin', you'd still look larra-pin' if you wore a flour sack, but if you want that dress, I want you to have it."

She shook her head. "Too impractical."

"And you're always practical?"

"Usually."

A few minutes later they were installed in a suite twice as big and considerably more garish than the tastefully appointed one they'd had in Dallas. Susan was reminded of a Victorian bor-dello.

While the bellman stowed their bags, she whispered, "Why do I have the impression that the bedrooms will have gold tassels on the bed-posts, mirrors on the ceilings, and that any moment the madame will come out?"

Ross laughed and tossed his hat on a huge bronze statue with a clock in her middle. "Think of it as an adventure, darlin'. You've probably never spent the night in a cat house before."

She cocked an eyebrow. "And *you* have, I suppose?"

"Not since I was a freshman in college and a bunch of us got tanked up on beer and visited the Chicken Ranch."

"The *Chicken* Ranch?"

"Sure. Didn't you ever see 'The Best Little Whorehouse in Texas'? It was based on a real place just outside of La Grange. I think once somebody raised chickens there, but when the ladies moved in, hell raising took over until a dogged TV reporter ran them out of business. Shame too. The Chicken Ranch was an old tradition."

Sticking her nose in the air, she said, "I really don't know much about such things, but I'm sure you had a wonderful time."

He laughed. "I don't think so. The last thing I remember is throwing up on some lady who wore a red negligee and too much makeup. I passed out on a couch and had to call my brother to pick me up the next morning."

"Paul?"

"Nope. Holt. I can't remember why he didn't go with us."

She sniffed. "Probably had too much sense."

He chuckled. "Probably."

A knock came at the door, and when Ross answered it, a waiter wheeled in a linen-draped trolley laden with flowers, iced champagne, and several bowls and plates of luscious looking fruit and canapés.

"Compliments of Mr. Green, sir," the waiter said, showing Ross the wine before he opened it.

Susan thought Ross seemed very blasé about the whole thing, but her eyes widened when she saw the Dom Perignon label. Though no connoisseur—her favorite wine had a screw-on cap and came from the grocery store—even she recognized bottled gold.

When the bellman and the waiter were gone and they sat together drinking the fancy champagne from fluted crystal glasses, Susan asked,

"Why do you rate VIP treatment here? Your brother again?"

Ross shook his head and grinned. "Naw, babe. Paul doesn't have a thing to do with this. I'm one hell of a poker player. I've won a few tournaments here and in Vegas."

"You're a *gambler*?"

"Hon, it's not gambling when it's a sure thing. I'm damned good."

"And modest, too. But you must have lost a bundle if Mr. Green is so glad to see you here. He was almost salivating."

"I rarely lose at poker. Born lucky, I guess. But, you're right, Marty likes having me around."

She frowned. "That doesn't make sense. Why would he want you here if you usually win?"

He grinned and kissed her nose. "Because I'm so purty?"

"Ross! Be serious."

"How about because I'm a colorful character who'll attract some high rollers who want to play against me?"

"Ohhh, I see," she said. "But we're not here for you to play poker. We're here only to find Mary Alice and get a lead on her mother."

"But Marty doesn't know that."

"Is that honest?"

He seemed amused by the whole thing. "Don't worry about it, hon. If we have time, I'll sit in on a couple of hands with some of Marty's big boys. If not, I'll catch them next trip. Things even out."

"But, Ross, how can you afford to play in high stakes poker games on a Ranger's salary? Even I know that some of those games can get awfully rich. Why, I'll bet that the pots can get higher than a year's pay."

He rubbed his nose against hers and nibbled on her lower lip. "Don't worry your pretty little head about it." He kissed her gently, and she could taste wine on his tongue. Strangely, the warm remnants of champagne tasted different in his mouth than in hers.

He plucked the glass from her hand and set it on the end table, then gathered her into his arms and kissed her again. His hand slipped up her stockinged leg and she shivered. Perhaps it was the wine, perhaps it was the man, or the potent combination of the two, but her defenses started to melt like marshmallows in hot cocoa.

The phone rang and she started.

"Let it ring," Ross said, nuzzling his way down her throat.

"But it might be about Mary Alice."

Ross spat out a succinct epithet, then answered the phone. Susan's anticipation quickened when she realized that Marty Green was on the phone. Impatiently, she waited while Ross asked a few questions, made notes, and hung up.

"Well?"

One corner of his mouth curved into a slow smile. "She was hired. She starts work as a coffee-shop waitress Sunday morning at seven. And the address personnel has for her is the Desert Rose Motel on Skyline Drive."

"Oh, doodle! That's the place I called last night. She's checked out."

He lifted her chin. "Don't let it get you down. We're getting closer. At least we know where we can find her at breakfast day after tomorrow.

Why don't we drive over to the Desert Rose and see what we can find out?"

They found out zip. Mary Alice had checked out two days before with no forwarding address. Waiting was their only option. They did a little sightseeing, which didn't take long in the small town, stopped for a snack at an interesting roadside cafe, then returned to the hotel.

Inside the lobby, the crowd had grown and the energy level had escalated. Susan lingered to watch a man feed silver dollars to a giant machine and pull the lever, then she ambled over to observe a senior citizen poking nickels into a machine festooned with grapes and watermelons.

"Want to try it?" Ross asked.

"Well . . ."

"I'll get you a roll of silver dollars."

"Silver dollars? No way. I think I have some nickels in my coin purse." She dug around until she found seven nickels. Ross turned on a light atop the machine while she fed three coins into the slot. She watched the cylinders spin, but nothing matched. She poked another three in, and when two bunches of cherries aligned, a bell rang and several coins fell into the trough.

"Oh, look," she squealed. "I won."

"You sure did, darlin'."

Breath held, excitement mounting, she tried another three nickels. Unfortunately, she fed all her winnings plus the coins from her purse into the slot with no additional return.

She sighed. *"C'est la guerre."*

Ross offered her two rolls of quarters he'd bought from an attendant. "Try your luck over there. I've got a good feeling."

Looking askance, she said, "Isn't that how people get suckered into losing fortunes? I think I'll limit my loss to thirty-five cents."

"Might as well try it, babe." He weighed the coin rolls in his hand. "These things are too heavy to carry around in my pocket."

Against her better judgment, she agreed. They scanned the quarter slots, trying to find the perfect machine, the one with the best vibes. She sat in various seats, and they studied the colors of the lighted panels until they decided on a blue one on the end. Ross broke the coins into a cardboard bucket and stood behind her as she started playing. She won and lost several times until her supply was down about half.

"I think this is a sucker game," Susan groused as she fed three quarters into the slot and punched the button to spin the cylinders.

Suddenly, bells went off like a fire alarm. Lights flashed and the machine went amok. Three colorful images had lined up across the face. An avalanche of quarters started spilling into the tray with a constant *ding, ding, ding.*

"Jackpot!" she shrieked, grabbing Ross and planting a big kiss on his mouth. "I hit the jackpot!" Jumping up and down, she pointed at the flood of quarters still falling into the receptacle. "Look, just look!"

He laughed. "Hon, there's lots more to come."

"More?"

"There wouldn't be enough room in the tray. An attendant will be here in a minute to pay you."

Her eyes wide as his words soaked in. "How much did I win?" she asked slowly.

He pointed to a wildly flashing sign overhead. When Susan saw the amount, she almost swallowed her tongue. Her hand flew to her heart. "Nine—" she croaked.

"—thousand, eight hundred and seventy-five dollars," he finished.

"Oh . . . my . . . Lord." Her knees buckled and she slumped against Ross.

By the time the floor manager reached them, a crowd had gathered to congratulate her. In a fog, she posed for photographs by the machine, then, still dazed, went with Ross and the floor manager to the cashier.

Ross nudged her gently. "Darlin', the man wants to know how you want your money. Cash, credit, or cashier's check?"

She tried to think, but her brain was still on overload. "You decide. Remember, half of it is yours."

"No, hon, it's all yours."

"But—"

"It's yours," he said emphatically. "Anything you want to buy that you'll need cash for?"

A wonderful, insane idea popped in her head. "Yes. I want to go shopping."

At Ross's direction, the cashier counted out several large bills, then cut a check for the remainder. Susan stared at the stack of cash in her hand. She'd never seen so many hundred dollar bills in her life. What if she were mugged? She grew more and more nervous thinking about it and glanced around, looking for suspicious characters.

"Ross," she whispered, "would you walk me to the boutique?"

"Sure. Want me to stay with you while you shop?"

She shook her head. "Nope. Just turn me loose and meet me in the room in two or three hours. I'll treat you to the fanciest place in town."

He laughed. "I'd better get my boots shined. Want me to make reservations?"

"Would you, please?"

"Your wish is my command, princess."

Two hours later, Susan, laden with packages, let herself into the suite. She called to Ross, but received no answer. Good, she thought, she'd have time for a leisurely bath before she donned her new clothes. One with bubbles. Lots of bubbles.

Humming to herself, she dumped her goodies on the bed, kicked off her shoes, and headed for the bathroom.

In a few minutes she had pinned up her hair and was leaning back in the deep marble tub amid froth up to her chin. She sang along with a soft rock tune on the radio, and lolled in the scented water. She felt positively decadent. This kind of life could be habit forming.

Still giddy from her good luck with the slot machine and her exorbitant shopping expedition, she lifted one leg high in the air and wiggled her red-tipped toes. She could hardly wait for Ross to see her in the blue spangled dress. It was the sexiest thing she'd ever owned. Thoughts of his reaction to her new outfit teased up other fantasies of the man who could turn her inside out with one of those smoldering, black-eyed looks. And kissing him was like sticking her finger in a light socket. That she hadn't thrown caution to the wind before now was a wonder. How much longer could she—

"You want some company?" a deep voice said from the doorway.

"Ross!" she squealed, instinctively crossing her arms over her body and scooting further beneath the bubbles. "I'm talking a bath!"

"Yes, ma'am." He grinned. "I noticed that right off."

"What are you *doing* in here?"

"Mostly looking at you and feeling like a dazed duck in a thunderstorm. I originally meant to tell you that we have reservations for dinner in an hour."

"You could have knocked."

"I did. Several times. I guess you didn't hear me." He ambled over and sat down on the corner of the tub. "Want me to wash your back?"

"Ross Berringer, you're shameless! Please leave."

He looked at her with a sort of amused indulgence. "Honey, I can't see a thing for all the bubbles. But I have to tell you that my imagination is kicking up a hell of a ruckus. Now, now, there's no need for you to get all bent out of shape about it. Sooner or later you're going to have to admit where we're headed."

She pursed her lips. "I'm sure I don't know what you're talking about."

He swirled his finger in the froth that seemed to be disintegrating at an alarming rate. "Sin, you and I were made for each other. And we're going to be so-o-o damned good when the kindling catches hold that we're gonna melt the bed springs. You won't be so modest then. I won't let you hide from me." His finger circled one knee that protruded from the bath. "I want to see all of you, feel all of you, smell all of you, taste all of you, and make love to you until these pretty little knees won't work."

Her heart lodged in her throat, and her skin suddenly seemed so hot that she was surprised the water wasn't simmering around her. Her first impulse was to drag him into the tub and say, "Have at it, big fella. I'm yours."

Fortunately, she had greater control over her hormones than to do such a foolish, impetuous thing. That was the sort of thing her mother would do. Instead, she masked her emotions and gave him her haughtiest glare. "Ross, I've told you that I'm not going to be another—"

"—notch on my bedpost," he finished. "Oh hell, darlin', forget all that bull corn about bedposts. You're the one for me, the only one. I know it, even if you haven't figured it out yet. Patience isn't my long suit, but I'll try to hold off until you come around." He smiled and tugged at a curl hanging on her forehead. "Now shake a leg, woman. I'm starving. And I'm anxious to see your new duds." He rose and sauntered out.

When she heard the door to her room close, she sat among the dissolving bubbles for a moment, pondering Ross's words. Were they simply a slick line or was there really something special between them? Was she falling in love with him? Could there truly be something permanent with Ross?

No, she told herself. She was merely suffering from a revved up libido. She might eventually have a fling with him, but love? She remembered all the times her mother had declared she was in love, sworn that this was IT. The feelings had been as ephemeral as the bubbles in the tub. Susan had read everything she could find on dysfunctional families, and hers had been a lulu. She understood the dangers of repeating those patterns, and she didn't plan to follow Barbara Bendel Weller Sinclair Bartlett Meers Guidry down that road.

Refusing to let thoughts of her mother dampen her spirits, she hurried out of the tub and dried off.

After winding the luxurious bath sheet around her, she applied her makeup, using the new tricks Linda had taught her. She spritzed on perfume and retouched her hairdo with the curling iron, then pulled on new pantyhose in a shimmery silver the clerk at the boutique had declared a must with the dress. She took the blue beaded confection from the box and slithered into it. Fully lined and with a sort of a built-in bra, the dress supposedly needed no undergarments, but she felt almost naked. The sensuous feel of silk across her bare nipples sent ripples over her skin.

Beginning to have second thoughts about her extravagant purchase, she studied herself in the full-length mirror, turning first to the right, then to the left. She'd feel better with a bra at least. But the spaghetti straps and the low back made an ordinary bra impossible, and she didn't have a strapless one with her. A long scarf had come with the outfit; maybe if she—

A knock at the door startled her. "About ready?" Ross called.

"Two minutes," she answered.

"You are going to wear the dress as is," she lectured her reflection. "If you've got it, flaunt it." She stuck out her chest and flung her hair over her shoulder with a quick toss of her head.

She fastened dangling crystals in her ears and stepped into new silver sandals with higher heels than she usually wore. As she stuffed a few essentials into an evening bag, she prayed that she wouldn't fall on her face and make a complete fool of herself.

Taking a last glance in the mirror, she felt a terrible sinking start in the pit of her stomach. Who was she trying to kid? She'd never been a glamour puss. Ross would probably think she was overdressed and ridiculous. She wanted to hide under the bed.

As if he could read her thoughts, he knocked again. "Come on out, sugar. I'm chomping at the bit to see you."

She took a deep breath, squared her shoulders, and opened the door.

Ross stared at her as if shocked. Panic scrambled up her throat. He let out a low whistle, and a slow smile spread across his face. As his eyes glittered like black jets, her confidence soared.

"Turn around, darlin', and let me get the full effect."

She slowly pivoted. "Do I look okay?"

"Hooo-wee, Sin, if you looked any better, I'd have a heart attack."

Noting his dark suit, white shirt, and tie, she said, "Do you think I'm overdressed?"

His eyes went to the bare expanse of skin over the bodice, and his grin widened as he ducked his chin. "Uh, no, I wouldn't say that."

Her confidence plummeted. She splayed her

hand across her chest. "I-I have a scarf. Or I can change."

He stepped close to her and pulled her hand away. "Susan Sinclair, love of my life, you're perfect. Absolutely, posi-damn-tively, gawl durned perfect."

"You're sure?"

"I've never been surer of anything in all my days. I may have to fight a few men off with a stick, but"—he kissed the cap of her shoulder—"what the hell? I always say, if you've got it, flaunt it."

She laughed. "Great minds."

He frowned, questioning her comment.

"Never mind," she said, hooking her arm through his. "I'm starved."


They sat at a secluded table in an elegant supper club where a piano played slow, tinkling tunes, eating caviar on toast points and sipping champagne that tasted like liquid sunshine. Ross winked at her. "Hell of a nice place not to have nachos."

A bubble of laughter slid up her throat, and she masked it with a sip of wine. "You're incorrigible."

He feigned wide-eyed innocence. "Isn't that what a cardboard box is?"

The laugh escaped. "You know very well what incorrigible means. I'm on to your game. You're not the 'aw, shucks,' uneducated redneck you'd like everybody to believe. I heard you order in flawless French."

"Well, my mama did insist that her boys learn a few of the niceties in life. We weren't always willing pupils either, but Miss Eleanor is a war-horse."

"I'd like to meet this formidable woman some-time."

"Count on it. And I guess sooner or later I'll have to parade Paul and Holt and Cory for your approval."

Surprised, she said, "My approval of your family isn't important."

"Sure it is, hon. There's a place at the Berringer table just waiting for you—for Thanksgiving or Christmas, stuff like that. My family has always been big on holidays. We'll include Dagna. She and my mother will hit it off great."

Growing uncomfortable with the turn of the conversation, she steered their talk in another direction. While they dined on exquisite French cuisine, they talked about a dozen things from what seemed to be an endless well of subjects they both enjoyed. And Ross, as usual, kept her entertained with his down-home humor.

She enjoyed being with him, listening to his deep voice, watching his eyes crinkle into dark quarter moons and the brackets deepen in his cheeks when he laughed—which was often. She liked the rugged planes of his face and his strong features. She liked the sensuous curve of his lips and remembered how they felt on her mouth, on her skin. A yearning ache throbbed low in her body and pulsated outward. Try as she might, she couldn't control the desire that swelled inside her.

"Babe," he said, his voice a hoarse whisper, "if you don't stop looking at me like that, the folks in this fancy French eatery are going to get quite a show."

Embarrassed, she said haughtily, "I'm sure I don't know what you're talking about."

"Yes you do. I'm gettin' hotter than Hannah's hairbrush, and all I can think about is making love to you on top of that piano."

Her eyes widened. "Ross! You shouldn't say things like that."

"Why not? It's the truth."

Heat blossomed over her face, and she focused her attention on the fork-tender veal in her plate, sawing on it as if it were a two-dollar steak.

Ross's hand covered hers to still it. "Hon, I'm sorry if I embarrassed you. I try to keep a bridle on my mouth, but things keep slipping the harness. I swear I'm not going to push you anymore. Okay?"

She nodded.

When the meal was done, Susan insisted on paying the check as she'd promised. She could tell it made Ross squirm, but she stuck by her guns.

As they left the restaurant, Ross said, "Would you like to see a show? We can see a review with lots of leggy girls, a comedy team that's supposed to be good, or Carly Simon."

"*Carly Simon*? Oh, Ross, could we? I adore Carly Simon."

"Darlin', when you smile like that, I'd lasso the moon if you wanted it and lay it at your feet."

Strolling back to their suite after the show, Susan felt as if she were walking on acres of fleecy cotton. Her arm around Ross's waist and his around hers, she rested her head on his solid shoulder and hummed one of the songs from the show. This night had been perfect—better than perfect. She hated for it to end.

It didn't have to end, she reminded herself. She was only punishing herself by denying what they both wanted. And she did want him, desperately. Her thoughts were obsessed by him, and her stamina to withstand his advances was flagging. Tonight when he pushed, she wouldn't resist.

Inside the suite, they found a midnight snack waiting for them—fruit, cheese, and another bottle of wine.

"Want some?" Ross asked.

She shook her head and stood waiting for him to kiss her. She didn't have to wait long. He took her into his arms and covered her mouth in a soul-stealing kiss that sent shivers meandering up and down her back. She gave herself over to the delicious feeling swirling inside her, and returned his kiss with all the pent up longing straining against its bonds.

He kissed his way down her throat and, with a flick of his thumbs, disposed of one thin strap, then the other. When his tongue drew a damp circle around the top of one bare shoulder, she clutched his coat to keep from slithering into a mindless puddle at his feet.

He peeled the bodice of her dress down to expose her bare breasts and groaned as her nipples became taut. "Perfect," he murmured.

Sinking into a nearby chair, he pulled her into his lap and kissed each swell reverently. When he took her nipple into his mouth, laved it, gently suckled it, wondrous sensations tingled her nerve endings. Her head dropped back, and she drew in a shuddering breath savoring the exquisite feelings bursting into flame. His mouth became hot and hungry, his hands urgent, his low growls exciting.

Would they go to her bedroom or his? Her room was a mess; she'd left stuff scattered everywhere. What about birth control? She didn't carry condoms in her purse. Was he prepared? What if he thought she was a lousy lover? After all, she wasn't as experienced as he was. One didn't call a quick tussle in the backseat of a car and five years of marriage to deadly dull Thomas Rowe experience. He was bound to be disappointed. She stiffened.

Ross's mouth ceased its marvelous torture, and he pulled back. His hands trembled as he carefully restored her bodice and straps. She was bewildered.

"Sugar, I'm sorry. I got carried away again after I told you— Anyway, I'm sorry."

"But, Ross—"

"Until you're ready, I won't push."

"But, Ross—"

"No, buts about it. I didn't mean to come on like a stallion at mating time." He patted her bottom. "Now you run on to bed. Sorry I can't escort you to your door, but I may walk funny for a while."

She hurried from the room, closed the door and leaned against it. So much for her wild, unbridled night of passion. She felt like the last child chosen on a baseball team. And sexually frustrated to boot.

Dejected, she undressed and scrubbed her face. What had gone wrong? She hadn't pulled away; he had. Maybe he didn't really want her. Maybe this was some sort of game.

No. She'd felt the evidence of his desire as she'd sat on his lap. He'd wanted her all right. Then what had happened?

Maybe he really was trying to be considerate of her feelings and not rush her. She wanted to march into his bedroom and scream, "Rush me! Rush me!"

Wait a minute. She'd taken a very passive attitude in their kissing and loveplay. Waiting for him, *allowing* him. By damn she was a liberated woman! How dare he?

She'd show Sergeant Ross Berringer a thing or two.

Furious with the turn of events and fired with resolve, she snatched up her new, very sexy black nightgown from one of the shopping bags and put it on. She spritzed a bit of perfume and walked through the mist. Before she lost her nerve, she stalked across the parlor to his room, stopping only long enough to grab a sharp knife from the fruit tray as she sailed past.

# *Eight*

His eyebrows rose when she opened the door. "You planning to stab me or geld me with that paring knife?"

The lamp was on, casting a dim glow across the big bed where Ross lay. As before, the cover only came to his waist. His bare chest was dark against the white sheets, and the silky thatch of hair that swirled over his well-developed pectorals caught the light and shimmered from black to bronze.

"Neither." She held out the knife to him. "It's to make the notch on your bedpost." Her voice sounded funny and quivery. She cleared her throat.

His eyes never leaving her, he took the knife and flung it into a corner where it hit the wall with a loud thump. "I'm out of the notch-making business, but I'd damn well like to make love with you, Susan. My heart and at least three other major organs are yours to command. Are you sure about this?"

She nodded. "Very sure. Are you . . . prepared?"

He chuckled. "Sin, I've been prepared since the first day I saw you. If you're not serious about this, you'd better run like hell because with that gown you're wearing, right now my molars are about ground to the gum."

"No, I mean . . . prepared. "Uh . . . you know . . . *prepared.*"

Amusement played around his mouth. "Ohhh, *prepared.*" A grin broke across his face. "You don't have to worry about a thing. Come here."

With a rustle of sheets, he pulled her down beside him. Very gently he kissed each of her eyelids, then the trembling corners of her mouth. "Are you nervous, sweetheart?" he asked.

"Maybe a little. I've never been very good at this sort of thing. I'm afraid you'll be disappointed."

"Not a chance."

Propped on one elbow, he kissed and caressed her with long, slow strokes until a sensual languor stole over her. Eyes closed, she savored the sensations aroused by his lips and tongue and fingers. He deftly disposed of her nightgown and turned his attention to her breasts, nipping and flicking his tongue over the sensitive tips, cupping their fullness in his hands.

While he kissed and suckled and rubbed his cheek across the delicate skin of her breasts, his hand smoothed its way down her rib cage, over the curve of her hip, circling her thigh, moving closer and closer to the juncture that ached with longing. The ache grew more intense as he teased her thighs apart ever so tenderly.

His tongue made a wet trail down her breastbone and circled her navel. His fingers made a foray that stole her breath and opened her eyes. That was when she saw it.

"Ross!"

"Hmmm," he replied, never ceasing his wondrous exploration.

"There's a mirror in the ceiling!"

"Um-hmm."

"Turn off the lamp."

"Uh-uh. I want to see you, and I want you to watch what I'm doing."

He was all over her, tasting, kissing, stroking like a man possessed. She tried to keep her eyes clamped shut, but they popped open in prurient fascination. Not only could she feel every brain-fogging sensation, but she could watch as he performed magic on her body. It was immensely erotic, surprisingly titillating.

He kicked away the cover and rubbed his tanned, muscular body against her lighter one with the fluid grace of a panther. She watched as his dark head moved over the surface of her skin, tasting, probing, robbing her of reason until she was writhing like a wanton. Moaning, she threaded her fingers through his hair and pulled his face to hers.

"What are you doing to me?" she asked, her voice a desperate whisper.

"I'm loving you like I've dreamed of doing, darlin'. I want to make your knees weak with wanting me."

Her breath caught in her throat. "I'm well past that stage. Well past."

"Not yet, darlin', but close."

His lips, firm and knowing, moved over hers with a hunger that sent a shock wave of desire rushing through her. As his hands stroked her body and his tongue plunged into the depths of her mouth, her inhibitions crumbled and her self-control burned to cinders. She made a tiny sound in the back of her throat and went wild.

Her hands ran over his damp body in brazen abandon; she met each thrust of his tongue with a demanding one of her own. She rooted her face against his neck, breathed in his masculine smell, licked his shoulder and savored the salty taste of his skin, dug her fingers into his back and begged him to fill her, complete her.

His breathing ragged, he moved away for a moment, then returned. She opened to him, reached for him.

He knelt and lifted her hips with a scoop of his broad hands. She clutched his shoulders and urged him to enter, but for a moment he only looked at her, his features a black-eyed portrait of smoldering expectancy, raw and passion-washed. "Do you want me to stop?"

"No. Lord, no," she groaned.

"If I go on, Susan, I'm branding you as mine. Do you understand?"

Restless with desire, she nodded.

"Say it then. Say you're mine."

"I'm yours. Only yours."

"Oh, babe," he moaned, driving swiftly and deeply into her. "Oh, love."

Her legs encircled him, corralled him, and their lovemaking became a torrent of churning desire, a maelstrom of erotic striving, a turbulent, spinning whirlwind. Their joining was primal, self-indulgent, yet at the same time a shared, consuming need to blend, to merge, to leap together into the brilliance of binding, blinding obsession.

As her passion grew to unbearable dimensions, Susan cried out in frantic, restless need.

"Easy, babe," he murmured. "Easy. I'll take you there." His hand slipped between them to stroke her gently with his thumb.

Immediately, she burst into wonderful, shattering golden spasms that seemed to go on and on and on. "Ross, oh, Ross."

Her words and her fulfillment seemed to splinter his control. He went rigid and a deep cry ripped from his throat.

For long moments, they lay intertwined, enjoying the afterglow of their lovemaking. Then he rolled to one side and tucked her against him. He laid his cheek on her forehead and ran his hand over the contours of her body.

"You are perfect, love. Absolutely, posi-damntively, gawl durned perfect. I knew we'd be hell on wheels in bed."

She laughed. "I didn't know I was such a wanton. You seem to bring out a part of me that I didn't even know existed."

He kissed her. "It's always been there . . . just waiting for me." He kissed her again. "Hungry?"

"A little."

"Be right back."

Totally unselfconscious of his nudity, he slipped from the bed. Susan stretched and watched him go, admiring his long torso, the curve of his lean buttocks, the length of his muscular legs. Catching sight of her own nudity in the mirror overhead, she scrambled for her gown and pulled it on.

In a moment he was back carrying the tray filled with wine, cheese, and fruit. He stopped and frowned. "Why did you do that?"

"Do what?"

"Put on your nightgown. Are you cold?"

She flushed slightly and shook her head. "I'm not accustomed to running around in the altogether."

"Better get used to it, babe. I plan to keep you that way—a *lot*." He skinned the satin and lace bit of capriciousness over her head and tossed it aside. Grinning, he tweaked her nose and popped a grape into her mouth. "And next time, *I* get to watch in the mirrors."

They slept late and ordered room service, then decided to drive to Lake Tahoe for the day. Reminding her that it would be cold in the higher elevations, Ross bought a wool sweater at the hotel men's shop, and Susan wore a similar one that she'd bought for Dagna on her shopping spree.

With Ross driving a rented car, a Lincoln this time—his long legs, he reminded her—they left the high desert for the mountains. The scenery was spectacular. A light snowfall a few days before had left patches of white on the tall evergreens along the winding road.

They parked at several places along the way to view the vast sweep of the Sierra wilderness, more majestic and breathtaking than anything Susan had ever seen before now.

"Oh, Ross, it's so beautiful," she said, her teeth chattering as they stood high in the mountains, looking down at miles and miles of lush green expanse below. Wonderful mountain streams tumbled over stones worn round and smooth by years of washing.

He hugged her close and rubbed her arms. "You're freezing. Let's get back in the car."

"I didn't realize my blood was so thin from living in Texas. And it isn't even winter yet."

At a quaint little trading post, they bought souvenirs and Ross found them each a wool poncho with an Indian design and a pair of gloves for her.

"I'm going to look like a bag lady when I get on the plane with all the extra stuff I've bought."

"Yep." He kissed her cold nose. "But you're going to be a warm bag lady."

After a wonderful day, they drove down from the Sierras to Reno as dark was beginning to fall.

At the hotel, they took a bubble bath, together this time. They drank more of Marty Green's champagne and cavorted like children—or lovers—in the huge tub.

They dressed and went to dinner, then wandered through the casino, trying their luck at various games, dancing to a band in one of the lounges. They caught the late show and laughed at a pair of comedians who entertained the audience with slightly risqué, but very funny, material.

Arm in arm, they strolled along the carpeted hall toward their room. "Tired?" Ross asked.

"A little. But a good tired." She leaned her head against his shoulder and yawned.

"Now don't do that. I hadn't planned on our going to sleep for a while."

They didn't. In fact, neither of them slept much. Ross was fascinated by the mirrors.

At nine-thirty Sunday morning, Ross and Susan walked into the coffee shop. He was wearing jeans, a faded denim jacket, and his black hat. She wore new designer jeans and a matching hand-painted jacket along with a spanking new pair of red western boots with butterflies on the shaft.

They'd meant to arrive earlier, but in the shower that morning, one thing had led to another, and . . . well they were later going downstairs than they intended.

Delicious smells of coffee and bacon and fruit wafting from the tables and the kitchen made Susan's tummy curl in anticipation. They'd had coffee in the room, but she was eager for another cup, and she was absolutely famished. Being hungry seemed strange since she rarely ate much breakfast.

Rush hour apparently over, several tables were empty, and Ross asked the cheerful hostess to seat them at Mary Alice's table.

The hostess cocked her head and frowned. "Mary Alice?" After a pause, she added, "Oh, the new girl. This way please."

Black ponytail bouncing, she led them to a table set for four. Amid the salt and pepper shakers, sugar packets, and syrup pitcher was the standard cut-glass bud vase with a single red carnation and one piece of fern stuck in it. Even though it was in an opulent hotel, the place seemed a clone of thousands of coffee shops around the country. It struck Susan as a very ordinary spot for the big confrontation they'd worked so hard for.

After Susan had perused the menu, she whispered, "I've got butterflies in my stomach. I don't know if it's because I'm so hungry or because we're about to meet Mary Alice."

Ross chuckled. "Maybe a little of both. I think I could handle a tall stack of pancakes along with three eggs, sausage, and biscuits."

They watched a young slip of a woman serve a tray of food to a table near them, then start their way, order book in hand. She wore a yellow uniform, which did nothing for her sallow complexion.

"This must be Mary Alice," Susan whispered from the side of her mouth. Try as she might to keep calm, her heart began to pound and her palms went damp.

The waitress reached for the pencil stuck in the careless knot of lank brown hair atop her head. Her face seemed drawn and her eyes looked older than the late twenties Susan suspected she was. Her fingernails were chewed to the quick.

The smile she gave them didn't quite make it to her darting hazel eyes. "What can I get for you folks this morning?"

"Are you Mary Alice Whiteside?" Ross asked.

Wariness registered in her eyes. "Yes," she answered timorously.

Ross pulled aside his jacket to reveal the silver star pinned to his shirt. "Ross Berringer, Texas Rangers. Ma'am, we'd like to ask you a couple of questions if you don't mind."

Panic flew across her face. She whirled and

bolted toward the kitchen like a frightened mouse.

"Come on," Ross said to Susan. "We've got to catch her."

They both jumped up and ran after Mary Alice, dodging tables as if they were on an obstacle course. They must have bumped a few, judging from the disgruntled shouts behind them, but they didn't slow to assess damage or apologize.

With Susan close on his heels, Ross charged through the swinging door to the huge kitchen. A dozen or more white-coated cooks working at various tasks stared at Ross and Susan as they started inside.

"You can't come in here!" a plump man in a tall hat screamed.

"The hell I can't," Ross yelled back. He grabbed Susan's hand and lunged forward. "This way. She went out the back."

As they zigzagged through the kitchen, the room turned chaotic. People cried out and tried to head them off, flapping aprons as if they were trying to herd chickens. Others jostled them, waved pots threateningly or tried to grab them. Susan's arms were nearly wrenched from their sockets with one angry cook on one end and Ross on the other, pulling her like a wishbone.

"Ross," she wailed.

He spun and stepped into a big stainless steel bucket of fish entrails someone had slid into his path. He let out a curse as he shook the mess from his boot. Glowering at her captor, he pulled his gun. "Security," he growled. "Let us through."

The room grew quiet, and her arm was freed.

He kicked the bucket to one side with another blistering oath and grabbed Susan again.

By the time they were out the back door, a screech of tires sounded from the parking lot on their right. An old blue Mustang was maneuvering quickly through the lanes of parked cars and headed toward them.

"This way," Ross yelled, steering her to the front of the hotel.

Mary Alice sped past them as they reached a row of taxis at the entrance. Ross commandeered the closest one, brushing aside a man with a suitcase.

"Emergency," he muttered in the way of an apology. The man with the suitcase gaped at the gun in Ross's hand and backed away. "Follow that blue Mustang!" Ross shouted to the driver as he jumped into the back seat, dragging Susan inside with him.

"Hot damn!" the driver said, flashing a gold-toothed smile. "I've always wanted to do this." He slapped the meter and burned rubber while Susan was still trying to close the door. She was almost thrown out of the cab.

Ross yanked her back in and slammed the door shut. "An extra fifty bucks if you catch her," Ross said to the cabbie as he holstered his gun.

"You got it, man. She ain't gonna lose me." The taxi ran a caution light and tore after the blue car, which was about a block ahead. "You two the law?" the driver asked.

"Yep."

"God will get you for all the lies you've been telling," Susan hissed in Ross's ear. He only winked and grinned.

"That gal we're chasing, did she rob somebody or something?" the driver shouted over his shoulder.

"Naw, we just need to question her about a case we're working on."

The cab whipped around a corner, and Susan, scrambling for a hold, slid against the door. Ross dragged her back against him and held her waist as they skidded through a series of sharp twists and turns. She felt like a passenger in the Indy five hundred.

"Hold on," the driver yelled. "Short cut."

He barreled through a parking lot and hit every speed bump doing fifty miles an hour. Their heads banged on the roof, then their bottoms slammed against the sprung leather seats as the taxi seemed to fly over the rough course.

"Lookie there," the driver—Roscoe P. Davis according to his license—crowed. He tore out of the lot right on her tail as Mary Alice sped out of town. "What do you want me to do now?"

"Stay on her until you find a deserted spot and force her over," Ross told him.

But fate intervened. The dented blue clunker slowed, then coasted to a stop on a deserted stretch of asphalt bounded by rough, sandy hills. Ross leaped out and ran to the Mustang; Susan was two steps behind. Wind from the high desert country whipped Susan's hair, tugged at Ross's hat, and flung grit in their faces.

Mary Alice sat cowed behind the wheel, shaking. "I'm not letting you take my babies."

Ross frowned and leaned down, resting his hands on the window opening. "Your babies?"

"Didn't my husband set you on me?"

"Rodney?"

"Yes," Mary Alice said, her voice quivering. "I've left him, and as soon as I can afford it, I'm getting a divorce. He's not going to punch me or those kids again."

"I don't blame you," Susan said, indignant at the idea of family abuse. "You don't have to put up with that kind of uncivilized behavior."

Mary Alice's hazel eyes darted between Ross and Susan. "If it's not about Rodney, then what do you want with me?"

"Just a couple of questions about your mother," Ross said, assuming responsibility for the interrogation.

Roscoe had heaved his considerable bulk from the cab and leaned on the front fender of the taxi, eavesdropping shamelessly.

"My *mother?*"

"Yes, ma'am. What's your mother's name?"

"Her name? Velma Henson."

"Do you know of her whereabouts?"

"The last I heard she was taking care of some old lady down close to Beaumont. I think she broke her hip—not Mama, the old lady."

"She's no longer employed there. You haven't heard from her in the past few days?"

Mary Alice shook her head. "What's this about? Has something happened to Mama?"

Ross cleared his throat. "Not exactly. Can you give us information about friends or relatives who might help us locate her?"

"I'm not telling you another word until you tell me what's going on. I don't think a Texas Ranger has any authority in Nevada." She clamped her lips shut and narrowed her eyes.

Susan spoke up. "The old lady your mother was staying with was my grandmother. Your mother left without warning last Tuesday and took several valuable items from the house."

Mary Alice's face crumpled and tears welled up in her eyes. "Oh, Lordy mercy. She told me she was through with that kind of thing. I'll bet Lon Yarrow's behind this. That man's the scum of the earth, worse than Rodney, a damned parasite always up to no good. Mama swore to me that she wasn't going to have anything more to do with him. Now look what she's gone and done."

Once the dam opened, Mary Alice told everything she knew. Her mother had been convicted of theft in Dallas using a similar scam masterminded by her boyfriend, Lon Yarrow. She'd been out of jail a few months and worked at a few temporary jobs using the name Maureen Potts, Velma's mother who had died a few years before.

"My grandma was an LVN, and even though Mama didn't have any formal training, she knew a lot about nursing. Natural like, you know. My daddy died in seventy-eight, not that either one of us missed his drinking and hell-raising much. Even though Mama worked hard and tried to keep a job, we lived on welfare mostly. I know she was lonesome, but she kept hooking up with a string of losers. That Lon Yarrow was no good at all. Damned blood sucker."

Ross asked several other questions, including a description of Lon Yarrow and anything about him she could remember. He noted her answers on a small pad he'd pulled from his pocket.

Mary Alice was extremely cooperative, and

while they learned a great deal about Velma Henson alias Maureen Potts, they learned very little about where to locate her.

"Oh, Lordy mercy," Mary Alice moaned, "I've probably lost my job now, and on my first day."

"Don't you worry about a thing, ma'am," Ross said. "I'll straighten it out with the hotel. You go on back."

"I can't. I'm out of gas. I was gonna use today's tips to buy some."

Roscoe and Ross left in the taxi to locate gas, and Susan scooted into the passenger side of the Mustang to stay with Mary Alice.

"Men!" The mousy woman spat out the word like poison. "I wouldn't give you a nickel for any of them. They're nothing but trouble. Oh, they say all the sweet sounding words to begin with. They'll lie and cheat and promise you anything—to get in your pants. But once the new wears off, they treat you like dirt and drag you down in the sewer with them. Look at the mess Mama's in. A man's behind it. But she's just gonna have to learn the hard way. I'm not hooking up with another one, no siree. I'm raising my babies and taking care of myself."

Susan asked about Mary Alice's children, and she took several pictures from her wallet, chattering about the two tow-headed youngsters.

Glancing through the pictures, Susan listened to Mary Alice's chatter with only half her attention. Mary Alice's vitriolic attack against men had set her thinking about dysfunctional families and the vicious circles of sick behavior people got caught up in. She'd done a lot of thinking about the subject since her divorce from Thomas. Susan's own parents had been as dysfunctional as Mary Alice's, and Mary Alice had fallen into the pattern of her mother.

Was she destined for the same trap? Susan wondered. Come to think of it, Ross did remind her a bit of her father, what little she could remember. They were both handsome, tall, masculine, robust, and could charm the birds from the trees—or any woman into their beds. Barbara had said that his lies and his philandering had broken up their marriage, but Barbara herself had a notoriously short attention span when it came to men.

No, she thought, Ross wasn't like her father. In many ways they were very different. But how well did she really know Ross? The gambling bothered her. Barbara's husband number three had been a gambler, not that Susan had known him very well. He hadn't cared much for children, and she'd stayed with Dagna during most of their short marriage. Barbara had told her that Mel Bartlett would gamble on anything, which was fine when they were in the chips. When he hit a long losing streak, Barbara left him before he could hock her mink.

Still, Ross seemed honest and sincere, nothing like Mel Bartlett who seemed to have the personality of a bottle cap. She smiled to herself. And Ross was a *fantastic* lover. As long as she didn't rush into anything or commit her heart to Ross, she'd be okay. Prudence was the key.

Her thoughts were interrupted by the return of the men with gasoline. While they funneled fuel into the Mustang, Susan took some bills from her wallet and tucked the money into Mary Alice's hand. The little waitress's eyes grew big. Susan said, "I want you to have it for anything you and the children need until you can get on your feet."

Tears streamed from Mary Alice's eyes, and she dashed them away with the tips of her chewed fingers. "I don't know when I'll ever be able to pay you back."

"I don't expect to be repaid. Just give someone else a hand sometime."

"I'm real sorry about what my mama did to your grandma."

Susan patted the woman's thin arm. "It's not your fault, Mary Alice. We can't help what our parents do, but we can try not to repeat their mistakes."

When the private jet was in the air and headed for Beaumont, Ross said, "I wish we could have stayed another night."

"But I have a business to run," Susan reminded him, "and I'm sure you have work to do. Besides, I want to check on Dagna and get right on the information we have on Maureen-Velma."

He nuzzled her ear. "You've talked to Dagna four or five times since we've been gone, and she's fine. As for the rest of it, we can't do anything until Monday. I'll get copies of Velma's record and check the motor vehicle division for a registration of an automobile for both her and Lon Yarrow. We might get lucky and find a current address."

"How long will that take?"

"A few days."

Susan sighed. "The longer we wait, the more unlikely that we'll find them or any of Dagna's stuff."

"We'll find them. You have to be patient."

She laughed. "*You* are telling *me* to be patient?"

He tossed his hat aside and pulled her into his lap. "That's what Holt always says."

"I'm going to have to meet this paragon."

"You will. Soon." He kissed her and rubbed his nose against hers. "Wanna join the mile-high club now?"

"Do I get a certificate?"

He grinned. "I'll have one specially made."

# Nine

Monday morning after following a hunch and doing some quick research, Susan dialed a pharmacy in Port Arthur, asked for a prescription refill, and recited the number off the bottle she'd scavenged from the garbage at Dagna's.

"Patient's name?" the druggist asked.

Susan crossed her fingers. "Velma Henson," she replied, trying to imitate Velma's nasal twang.

"Ms. Henson, I notice that your prescription was refilled only a few days ago. You should have a month's supply."

"Well," she said, stalling to think of an excuse, "I did have, but I had an accident. I—uh—it's those durned childproof bottles. I was trying to get the lid off and the whole thing flew out of my hands and pills went every whichaway. Most of them ended up in the toilet. A few of them landed on the floor, but I wouldn't want to take them *now*. Not sanitary, not sanitary at all."

"I understand, Ms. Henson, but be careful in

the future. Your prescription should be ready in about an hour."

"Thank you, I'll have my niece pick it up."

After hanging up, she slumped over the phone, her heart pounding in her ears. That was a close call. Too close. But the medicine bottle would provide some additional information: a doctor's name, maybe even an address. True, Ross had promised to check both Velma and Lon Yarrow's records, but that would take at least a couple of days, probably more with the way bureaucracy worked. Susan felt she had to do *something* in the meantime.

The phone rang and she answered it.

"Morning, sugar," Ross said. "I didn't wake you, did I?"

The afternoon before, shortly after they'd arrived back in Beaumont, Ross had an emergency call to report to Houston. Some kind of big Ranger doings with several men called in. He'd groused, but he'd gone.

"No, I've been up awhile. Where are you?"

"Still in Houston. Looks like I'm going to be here most of the day. Miss me?"

"I've been too busy to miss anybody. I was up until midnight catching up on paperwork. Nadine and her sister-in-law are going to run the bookstore again today, and I thought I'd go see Dagna. And maybe do some digging around," she added cautiously.

"What kind of digging?" His voice was wary.

"Oh, you know, checking out the phone calls Velma made from Dagna's, that kind of thing."

"Hon, I've told you to leave things to the professionals. I don't want you to bite off more than you can chew and get hurt."

"How can I possibly get hurt sitting here using my computer? Honestly, you're like a mother hen."

"Maybe so. But promise me you'll wait till I come home to handle things."

"What was the big emergency in Houston?"

He chuckled. "You know I can't talk about ongoing investigations. Promise me?"

Her attempt at diversion was a bust. "Ross, I'm an intelligent woman. I don't plan to do anything dangerous or stupid."

"See that you don't."

"Yes, sir, Mister Ranger, sir."

He laughed. "Now you got it."

"Dream on."

"Gotta go, babe. Somebody's yelling for me. See you tonight."

She didn't tell him about the pharmacy. Nor did she tell him she'd discovered that one of the numbers Velma had called on Dagna's phone was Fontenot's Bar, the same Port Arthur bar advertised on the matchbook she'd found in the garbage. She also neglected to mention that a pawnshop in Beaumont was the other number and that she planned to do some nosing around. He was such a worrywart.

She'd found it! Knees knocking, Susan got into her car and drove two blocks before she pulled over. She felt as if her heart were going to jump out of her chest. Taking several deep breaths, she tried to calm herself.

She'd just spent the last few minutes nosing around the pawnshop on her list. With a bit of sleuthing and subterfuge, she'd spied Dagna's precious stick pin in the sleazy store. That sorry piece of scum who owned the shop probably had lots of Dagna's other things as well. A dollar to a doughnut he knew the stuff was stolen. It had taken a monumental amount of control not to accuse the man of corrupt business practices and demand that he hand over the loot from Dagna's house. But that would have been class A dumb. If he'd become at all suspicious, he'd have stashed the stuff where it would never be found.

Should she call the cops? Which cops? The Beaumont police, who knew nothing about the case, or that idiot Leonard Bottoms who would screw things up? After giving the matter considerable thought, she knew the only thing to do was wait for Ross. Darn him anyway! Where was he when she needed him? Off on secret Ranger business.

She decided that while she was out, she'd drive to Port Arthur and pick up the prescription. She was a little nervous that the druggist might recognize her voice, but a woman was behind the counter.

Susan almost choked when the woman rang up seventy-four dollars for the medicine, but she kept a straight face and paid with the last of her hundred dollar bills. While the clerk was making change, Susan picked up the bottle. The doctor's name was listed, the name of the medication was neatly typed in the proper place, but there was no patient address. Doodle! Double doodle!

"Uh . . . my aunt wanted to check to see if you have her new address," Susan improvised. "She's recently moved."

"I'll check the computer. What's her new address?"

This wasn't working out as she'd planned. "Two twelve Benbrook Drive," Susan said, rattling off the address of a friend in Ohio.

"No, we have her listed on Hardy Street. I'll change it."

She itched to peek at the computer or ask what number on Hardy Street, but fearing that the whole thing would blow up in her face, Susan decided not to press for more information. Hardy street was a start and better than nothing. She mumbled her thanks and beat a hasty exit.

She stopped for gas and bought a city map. While she was in town, she might as well drive by Fontenot's Bar. Just drive by. She didn't intend to go in.

Daylight did nothing for Fontenot's Bar. It was a sleazy place in a seedy part of town. Nobody could have paid her to go in that place alone, even at high noon. Quite by accident, she discovered that Hardy Street was one block from the bar.

As she drove back to Beaumont to change clothes before visiting Dagna, an idea popped into her head. The minute she reached her town house, she telephoned Fontenot's Bar.

When a gruff voice answered, she pitched her own voice a breathy octave lower and asked, "Is Lon there?"

"Lon Yarrow? Naw, he don't come on till seven—if he decides to show up at all."

"Thanks." She hung up quickly and let out a whoop. Those two buggers were as good as caught.

• • •

Dead tired and looking forward to a shower and a decent night's sleep, Ross hit the city limits of Beaumont at a little before ten o'clock. He hadn't been to bed since Saturday night in Reno, and he hadn't slept a hell of a lot then, he thought, remembering with a grin.

Rubbing his eyes against the glare of headlights, he fought a yawn. He supposed he should have spent the night in Houston, but he was eager to get home and see Susan. Even if he only kissed her goodnight, he wanted the time with her.

Lord, she'd sure put his heart on a leash in a hurry. Even as busy as he'd been for the past thirty hours on a nasty kidnapping case, thoughts of Susan, pictures of her face and memories of the way she held her head when she laughed, popped into his mind every few minutes. She'd become an obsession. And he loved her more than he'd ever thought it was possible to love a woman. He loved her so much it made him feel as if he could take off and fly like an eagle.

Was it too soon to propose? he wondered. He sure as hell wanted to marry her—and right away. He wanted to love her and pamper her and give her the moon in a red ribbon. He'd never been one to let grass grow under his feet when his mind was made up. But Susan was more cautious. She'd given him the impression that, with her mother's track record and her own one bad experience, she wasn't too keen on matrimony. Not that they'd ever talked about it much;

it was just a feeling he had. He might have to do a little convincing.

Maybe he should trot out a good example of what a successful marriage really was. Holt and Cory's marriage was an extremely happy one. Yeah. He'd ask them down this weekend. Susan and Cory would hit it off great, and Ross wanted to see his twin.

He swiped his hand over his stubbled jaw and rolled the window down so that cool air blew across his face. Of course there were a couple of things that he and Susan needed to discuss, the major one being that he never did get around to telling her about the Berringer money. But that was no big deal. She'd understand.

Ross was relieved when he parked in front of the row of town houses a few minutes later. He dragged himself out of his pickup and went to Susan's door. He rang the bell, eager as a kid to see her pretty face.

No answer. He rang the bell again and waited, hat cocked back and weight against the jamb. Still no answer. Damn! Maybe she'd decided to spend the night with Dagna, or maybe she was visiting friends. He'd grab a shower and call her later.

Unlocking his own door he found an envelope taped at eye level. He ripped it off, went inside, and turned on a lamp to read the note. It was from Susan.

"Godamighty!" he roared. "She hasn't got the sense God gave a pissant! Surveillance? Hell, in that part of Port Arthur at night, alone, she'll be damned lucky if she doesn't get raped and her throat cut."

Fear and anger shot a jolt of adrenaline

through his bloodstream. Muttering strings of the most vile and colorful oaths he could splice together, he slammed the door hard enough to be heard in Dallas and stalked to his truck. In seconds, he was peeling down the street, tires smoking and heart racing like a Texas twister.

He made the twenty mile drive in fifteen minutes.

Her car parked in the shadows across the street and catercornered to Fontenot's Bar, Susan shifted restlessly behind the wheel and took a sip of the watery cola she'd bought hours ago. Even though she'd tightly wrapped the remnants of her meal and stuffed them into the bag, the onion and mustard smell of the cheeseburger permeated the car, growing more pungent by the moment.

She rolled down the window a crack and tried to fan the smell outside. It didn't help. Because the night was humid and the area close to the refineries, the odor outside was worse than the onions inside.

Stakeouts weren't nearly as exciting as they seemed on TV. If Ross were here, at least she'd have somebody to talk to, but she'd waited for him until almost seven. She'd tried to talk her friend Linda Brewer into coming with her, but Linda wasn't the adventurous type. Actually, Linda had said that the whole idea was nuttier than a fruitcake and dangerous to boot.

But it seemed logical to Susan that if Lon Yarrow worked at the bar and if Velma was enamored of him, she might drop by for a drink. If she did, all Susan had to do was follow her home to know where she lived. Unfortunately, Velma hadn't come by. A couple of dozen other people, mostly men, had come and gone, but no Velma.

Needing to use the ladies' room, she wiggled in the car seat and tried to ignore the urge. She knew that as soon as she left to find a service station, her quarry would show up. She kept her eyes on the bar's door.

What if Lon Yarrow hadn't reported for work? The man she'd talked to earlier had intimated that Lon wasn't always reliable. Wouldn't that be the pits? She could be sitting here being miserable for nothing.

The state of her bladder and a need to know if Lon really was inside germinated an idea. She could go in the bar, use the bathroom, and casually order a soft drink. Or maybe a beer would be better. Yes, definitely a beer. That way she would know for certain that Lon was there. She was sure to recognize him from Mary Alice's description: a heavyset man with very curly red hair going to gray, a thick mustache, and a cobra tattoo on the back of his right hand.

No, the whole idea was insane. A woman alone going into a bar like that was asking for trouble.

But no one had bothered her in all the time she'd been sitting here alone. Besides, she had a can of Mace in her jacket pocket.

She vacillated back and forth until she finally decided to go for it. Basic needs tended to make one take a few chances. Tucking her keys in a pocket of her shoulder bag, she eased out of her car.

Tall bushes around the nearby chain link fence formed dark grotesque shapes. The air seemed oppressively still. What if someone was hiding in the bushes, waiting for her? She glanced nervously over her shoulder.

A sudden, piercing yowl jarred her nerve endings. She sucked in a startled gasp, and her heart turned over. A cat, she told herself. Just a cat. But she gripped the Mace in her pocket and kept her finger on the button.

As she started to cross the street at a diagonal, hairs on the back of her neck prickled up. She could have sworn she heard footsteps behind her. She quickened her pace.

A big hand gripped her elbow and a deep voice growled, "Where the hell do you think you're going?"

Petrified, she screamed, whipped out the Mace, and gave a half squirt at the attacker before she recognized his voice. He let out a roar and followed it with a string of shocking oaths.

"Ross! Oh, no. Oh, dear, I'm so sorry. But I didn't know it was you."

He was bent over, his arm across his eyes, still cursing. In empathy, she screwed her face into a pained grimace to match his and wrung her hands.

"Ross, I'm so sorry. Oh, I'm so sorry. Here let me help you."

She tugged him back to her car and fumbled trying to unlock it. She yanked a handful of tissues from the box she kept in the backseat and dunked two bunches of them in the cola, which was the only cool liquid available. She patted his eyes and wiped his face with the soggy tissues, apologizing all the while.

"What in tarnation did you spray on me? It's burning like holy hell."

"Mace. Here, hold these tissues over your eyes. The burning will go away in a few minutes. I only gave a little squirt, and I don't think any got directly on you."

"I'd hate to know what a face full of it would feel like. My mouth and nose and eyes are burning like fire."

"I'll take you to an emergency room, and they can flush it out."

"I don't need to go to a damned emergency room, but if you can find a gas station with a water hose, I'd appreciate it."

A few blocks away, she located a station and wheeled in. But instead of using the water hose, he stalked to the men's room, tears streaming down his face.

Hurrying along behind him, she asked, "Don't you want me to help you?"

He glared at her from watery eyes. "Don't push it."

She shrugged and veered toward the ladies' room.

A few minutes later, she was sitting in the car waiting when Ross came out. The front of his shirt was wet and his eyes were red, but he looked much better. Except that the muscles of his jaw were jumping like bugs on a griddle.

"Are you okay?" she asked cautiously as he slid into the front seat.

"If feeling like I've had my head stuck in a bed of fire ants is okay, then I'm okay."

"Ross, I'm sorry you're angry, but I really didn't mean to hurt you. You startled me, and I simply reacted. You might have been a mugger."

He let out his breath with an exaggerated puff. "I know, sugar. And you did the right thing. I'm just dead tired, and I was worried sick about you. How did you come up with such a scatter-brained idea of a stakeout in the first place?"

Indignant, she pursed her lips and narrowed her eyes. "It was *not* a scatterbrained idea. It was an excellent idea."

"Sin, honey, if you'll be a little patient, I've contacted several agencies, and I should start getting back information any day now. Can we talk about this in the morning? I'm bushed."

Still irritated with his attitude, she drove him back to his truck. He insisted that she abandon her surveillance, and he drove behind her all the way to Beaumont to make sure she got home safely.

When she opened the door, he followed her inside.

"I thought you were tired," she said.

"Don't you know, sweet Sin, that I'm never too tired for you?"

He gathered her in his arms and kissed her, but, still miffed at him, she kept her lips tense. "I'm going to take a shower."

He kissed her eyelids and rubbed his nose against hers. "How about some company?"

"No, thank you very much. I'm not too scatterbrained to wash my own back."

"Aw, hell, honey, I—"

She shot him a look designed to stop a speeding train and stalked to the bathroom. When she came out a few minutes later, she found him stripped to his briefs and sprawled on her bed—sound asleep.

Fleetingly she considered the couch, then abandoned the idea. Instead she climbed into the small space his big frame didn't occupy and clung to the edge of the mattress.

She awakened the next morning with a hand cupping her breast and her bottom resting spoon fashion against a warm, virile body. Her breath caught, and she almost snuggled closer before she remembered that she was angry with Ross. Gingerly, she crept from the bed and dressed quietly. She wanted to be gone before he awoke. Scatterbrained, indeed! His words still stung.

She went to the store two hours early and threw her total concentration on paperwork that she'd neglected. Shortly after she opened The Great Escape for business, Ross sauntered in, all smiles and his hat shoved back. He carried a bundle of yellow spider mums, which he presented to her with a flourish and a kiss.

She didn't even pucker. She wasn't about to be bought off so easily.

"Darlin', I'm sorry I was such a jackass last night, but I hadn't slept since Saturday night. And, as I recall, not much sleeping went on then." He grinned. "But you have to know that you've become the most important thing in the world to me. I love you, honey, and the thought of you out on the streets in a rough part of town about scared the pea turkey out of me."

She went still. "What did you say?"

"I said that you about scared the pea turkey out of me."

"No, before that."

He grinned. "The part about me being a jack-ass?"

"No, after jackass and before pea turkey."

His face sobered, then turned tender. "I love you, honey. You're the most important thing in the world to me."

"I need to put these in water." She grabbed the flowers and fled to the back of the store.

Her hands shook as she fumbled through the lower cabinet looking for a vase.

"Need some help, Miss Turtle?"

She glanced up to find Ross squatting beside her. "Turtle? Why a turtle?"

"Because every time I get too close, you pull into your shell or skitter away like Bond or Moneypenny. Is it so awful that I love you?"

"Yes. No. Oh, I don't want to talk about it."

"See, you've proved my point. But I'll drop it for now." He gently kissed each eyelid, then the tip of her nose, then her lips. "I'll leave so we can both tend to business, but I'll take you someplace special for dinner tonight, okay?"

She nodded.

"And no more playing detective."

She didn't say anything.

"Susan, no more playing detective, okay?"

His smug manner irked her to no end. "It may interest you to know, Sergeant Berringer, that I've discovered where Dagna's stuff is, which is more than I can say for the *professionals* involved in the case."

She told him about her visit to the pawnshop and the pharmacy. "I'm pretty sure that Velma lives in Port Arthur on Hardy Street, probably with Lon Yarrow who works at Fontenot's Bar. The only thing I don't know is the exact address."

"Did you try the phone directory?"

"Of course I tried the phone directory. I also called information. No listing for either."

He pulled her to her feet, sat her on the counter, and kissed her again. His tongue made spine-tingling forays into her mouth that stole her breath and heated her blood. His touch reduced her to a panting mass of nerve endings. The distant sound of a tinkling bell abruptly halted their lovemaking.

"A customer," Susan whispered.

Ross took a deep breath and let it out with a soft whistle. "Woman, you ought to be illegal." He lifted her down from the counter. "I'll round up the bad guys for you, sugar. Trust me. I'll get in touch with both the Beaumont and Port Arthur police departments. Just be patient."

"If I hear that one more time, I may scream. I'm sick and tired of trying to be patient. If I'd been patient, we wouldn't know anything."

Two days later, Susan's patience was at the bottom of the barrel. She wanted to go outside and rip loose with a primal scream that would stop traffic. Instead she formulated a plan.

After calling Nadine to open the store for her, she dressed in one of her cotton shirtwaists with a Peter Pan collar and put on her espadrilles. She gathered a few props from her desk, then stopped by the drugstore and bought the tackiest pair of glasses she could find, ones that were little more than clear glass. At nine o'clock, she marched into Linda's beauty shop and asked to borrow a black wig.

"Why do you want a black wig?" Linda asked.

"It's part of my disguise."

"Susan, are you playing Sam Spade again?"

"Nope. Edward X. Delaney is more my style."

"Ross is going to have a cat fit."

"That's tough. Will you loan me a black wig?"

By ten o'clock, she was parked at one end of Hardy Street, which was, thank goodness, only ten blocks long. Most of the houses looked as if they'd been built just after World War II—and hadn't been painted since.

She patted her wig, grabbed her clipboard and pencil, and walked confidently to the first door.

A woman holding a baby on her hip and with a dirty-faced toddler hanging onto her skirt answered her knock.

"Good, morning," Susan said. "My company is doing a survey on pets. Do you have a pet in your household?"

# Ten

A few minutes before noon, Ross cruised down Hardy Street, trying to spot a black, eighty-nine Bronco with the license number he'd received from the DMV an hour ago.

There, that might be Lon Yarrow's truck in the carport.

He drove to the end of the block, turned his gray, state-issued car around and came back for a second look. This time he noticed a blond, middle-aged woman in unflattering stretch pants watering some scraggly flowers beside the house. Must be Velma. Yep, that was the place all right—2413 Hardy. The blonde tossed aside the hose and went inside.

He stopped a few houses away and radioed for the Port Arthur police to pick up the suspects. As he sat waiting, he observed a tall, black-haired woman in a pink dress going from house to house. She carried a clipboard and looked as if her feet hurt.

Eyes narrowed, he watched her walk up the

steps to 2413. There was something about her, about the way she carried herself that—

He jolted upright from his slumped position. *Good godamighty damn!* It was Susan.

His first impulse was to run across the street and drag her away from that place. Lon Yarrow had a sheet longer than his arm; he was one mean son of a bitch.

Ross forced himself to wait. His fingers bit into the steering wheel. Beads of sweat popped out on his forehead.

After what seemed like an eternity, but was only a couple of minutes, she came down the steps, gripping the clipboard with both hands. To give her credit, Susan didn't do anything suspicious. She walked to the house next door and spoke briefly to the person who answered. She did the same with the last two houses on the block, then turned the corner.

He started the engine and moved slowly away until he rounded the same corner and spied her sauntering along the sidewalk. Pulling to a stop, he threw open the door and stomped over to her.

"Get in the car," he growled at her.

She blinked twice behind the ugly horn-rimmed glasses she wore, and her back went as stiff as a branding iron. "I beg your pardon?"

"Hell, Susan, you nearly scared the spit out of me. Do you know who you were talking to back there?"

"Of course I know. Lon Yarrow and Velma Henson. Wasn't I just on my way to find a phone to call you?" She gave him a smug smile. "I found them—2413 Hardy. Velma had her roots touched up. She looks much better. Of course, I only got a peek, but I saw a half dozen or more

TV sets in the living room—ill-gotten gains, if you ask me—and there were boxes of stuff stacked everywhere. All hot, I'll bet anything. And did you know they have a cat?"

"I don't give a damn if they have a kangaroo. Get in the car."

Susan, eyes wide, looked him up and down. "My, my, my. Testy today, aren't we? Did somebody spit in your hat?"

He couldn't fight a chuckle. "I swear, woman, looking after you would be a full time job."

"I can look after myself, thank you very much. Aren't we going to call the police?"

"I've already called the Port Arthur PD. They're on their way."

She grabbed his hand and dragged him to the car. "Well, hurry up. If we keep standing here talking, we might miss the grand finale."

They almost did miss it. Ross pulled the gray sedan to a stop just as two uniformed officers brought Velma and Lon out of the house, handcuffed and sullen.

"Hot dog!" She made a pistol of her finger, pointed it at Velma, and fired an imaginary shot. "Gotcha!" Laughing, Susan plucked the wig from her head and shook her hair free. "Crime," she said to the rear of the police car as it pulled away, "doesn't pay."

She threw her arms around Ross and hugged him. "Let's go call Dagna, then we'll celebrate."

"I thought we were going to celebrate," Susan said, feeling lazy and replete. She lay in bed on her stomach while Ross nibbled his way up her backbone, vertebra by vertebra.

"But, babe, we've been celebrating." He blew on her back and made a vulgar sound.

She giggled. "No, I meant with fancy food and all the works."

"I brought champagne and nachos. And they were damned fine nachos. I made them myself."

Laughing, she turned over and, with the tip of her index finger, traced the tiny pink scar where his stitches had been. "Yes, they were damned fine nachos. I know I'll never be bothered with sinus problems again. But you shouldn't have spent your money on such expensive wine. It's one thing when it's free, but quite another—"

He pressed his fingers against her lips. "Uh, sugar, I've been meaning to tell you something about that. Right now money is the least of my worries."

Puzzled by his comment, she asked. "What do you mean?"

"I mean that my brother Paul isn't the only Berringer with money. None of the family is exactly hurting."

She grew still. "Are you trying to say that you're rich?"

"Well, I'm not another J. Paul Getty, but I inherited a share of the family holdings, and Holt and I have made a little more in oil and cattle."

"Do you have as much money as your brother Paul?"

Absently stroking her arm, he shrugged. "About that."

Shaking off his hand, she shot straight up and glared at him. "You *lied* to me." Feeling suddenly vulnerable, she gathered the sheet around her to cover her nakedness.

"Aw, hon, I didn't lie."

"If you didn't lie, you came damned close. You deliberately gave me the impression that Paul was rich and that you and Holt were merely ordinary folks."

"We *are* ordinary folks. Paul likes running the family business, my mother likes digging in her garden, and Holt and I like being Rangers. All of us eat fried chicken with our fingers and scratch when we itch. Most of the time I don't even think about having money. To tell you the truth, sometimes I'm embarrassed about it."

He started to kiss her, but she turned her face away. Her thoughts were in a turmoil. If she wasn't in her own house, in her own bed, she'd have her clothes on and be out the door in a flash.

"Sin, you're overreacting. My having money is no big deal. It doesn't change who I am or what's happened between us. You're not going to let this bother you, are you?"

"I don't know. I'll have to think about it. You'd better go now. I need some time by myself."

She kept her face to the wall, but she heard him sigh and felt his weight leave the bed. After a rustle of fabric, she heard his jeans zip. The bed dipped briefly, then shook, and she imagined him pulling on his boots.

Instead of leaving, those boots walked around to her side of the bed. Ross, shirt on but unbuttoned, sat down beside her. He took her chin in his hand and lifted her face until their eyes met.

"Another thing you might as well think about while you're hiding in your shell, Miss Turtle, is that I love you and I intend to marry you come hell or high water. Since I believe that you love me, too, even though you might not want to admit it, you ought to know that you can't run far enough or fast enough to get away from me."

He kissed her briefly, then added, "Don't forget I have a special dinner planned Saturday night at my place. Seven o'clock."

Her brain paralyzed, her chest tight, she stared at the flowers on the wallpaper. She didn't know how long she sat there dazed, smothering, clutching the sheet. Panic was the first emotion she felt.

*Marriage? Oh, Lord, no!*

She grabbed her clothes, threw a few things in a bag, and in fifteen minutes, she was on her way out of town. She ended up where she always ended up when she was troubled. In Vendor at Dagna's.

Essie was asleep, but Dagna was still up, watching Arsenio Hall. Susan tossed her bag in the bedroom everyone still called hers, pasted a smile on her face and strolled into her grandmother's room.

Dagna's laugh faded as Susan walked in. "Honey, what's wrong?"

"Why nothing's wrong, Dagna." She leaned over to kiss her grandmother's wrinkled cheek. "I just wanted to give you a firsthand account of the capture of Velma Henson alias Maureen Potts."

"But we talked about it on the telephone this afternoon. You gave me a blow-by-blow description of everything that went on. Did you leave something out?"

Susan shook her head. Her chest was hurting again.

"I tell you what. You go get us each a big bowl

of peppermint ice cream and by the time we finish it, maybe you'll tell me what's troubling you, pumpkin."

Susan smiled at the childhood nickname and started toward the kitchen. How many times had she and Dagna solved problems over a bowl of peppermint ice cream? Even the familiar ritual of scooping the pink stuff from the half-gallon carton was soothing.

She stuck a spoon in each mound, tucked napkins under her arm, and carried the bowls in Dagna's room.

Dagna patted the bed beside her, indicating Susan's place. Susan handed Dagna one bowl, kicked off her shoes, and settled Indian fashion on the eyelet coverlet.

Silently, each savored a few bites.

"Ross is rich."

"Ah." Dagna took another bite, then said, "How rich?"

"I'm not exactly sure, but I think extremely."

"So?"

Susan crunched a sliver of peppermint candy. "He wants to marry me."

"Well, good for him. I could tell right off that young man had a head full of sense."

"But, Dagna, I can't marry Ross. I can't marry anyone."

"And I'd like to know why not? Don't you love him?"

"Yes, I think I do, but it's not that simple."

"Sounds simple enough to me. He's a fine young man with good character. He loves you, you love him. What's the problem?"

"He gambles."

Dagna's pale brows rose. "Is it a sickness with him?"

"No, I don't think so. But he plays high stakes poker sometimes. You should have seen the manager fawning over us in Reno."

"Your grandpa used to play poker now and again—pretty good at it, too. And I've been known to wager on a game of chance. Seems to me you were telling me about winning a big jackpot on the slot machines, and I recall us going to the horse races a time or two." Dagna scooped up the last of her melting ice cream. "Is gambling really the problem?"

Susan stared at her empty bowl, then sighed. "No. I'm afraid that I'm going to be like Mother, and Ross is number two in a long string of husbands. I don't want to be like that, Dagna, and I won't subject children to such a life."

"Lordamercy, where did you come up with such an idea? You're nothing like Barbara. She's as flighty as a hummingbird, and you're as steady as a rock. Even though she's my daughter and I love her, Barbara's as shallow as a saucer of water. Your thoughts and feelings run well deep."

"But, Dagna, you don't understand. I come from a dysfunctional family and patterns tend to repeat themselves. Look at me, I've already had one failed marriage."

"Hogwash! Every magazine I pick up is yammering about dysfunctional families, and half the talk shows I watch on TV are spouting off about the same thing. If you ask me, the whole thing is a fad folks have latched onto to try to explain something nobody really understands and to blame their problems on somebody else.

Now I'm not saying that some parents aren't messed up and do real harm to their kids. I've seen it often enough. But you can't wallow around in the muck forever. There comes a time when a body has to shake off the past, take responsibility for herself, and get on with the business of living. Even with the bad start Jake Sayer's kids got, most of them turned out just fine."

"But—"

"But nothing. Tell me this—do you honest and truly think you're like your mother?"

Susan shook her head and set their bowls aside. "Linda says sometimes I bend over backwards to be totally opposite from her."

"You don't have far to bend."

"Linda also says that I run from deep emotional commitments with men."

Dagna nodded. "I've seen that."

"Sometimes Ross calls me Miss Turtle."

Dagna held out her arms and Susan snuggled close to her the way she once did as a child. "It pains me that Barbara's behavior has made you afraid to love." Dagna stroked her hair. "Now, marriage isn't always roses, and you have to work at it, but there's nothing finer than the deep, enduring love of a good man. I had that. I wanted it for Barbara, I want it for you. Ross is a good man, pumpkin. Trust your heart."

For a long time they were quiet, and Susan simply soaked up the love that was evident in every stroke of her grandmother's hand.

"Dagna, do you ever wonder why Mother is the way she is?"

The old woman continued her stroking. "Many's the time I've lain awake in this very bed, wondering what I could have done differently, worrying over her latest escapade. Your granddaddy and I loved her and did the best we could. From the time she was a baby, she never could be happy with anything for very long. She always had a restless spirit. I figure that some souls are just born to be the way they are." After a moment, Dagna added softly, "But once in a while it grieves me."

On Saturday morning, Susan drove to The Great Escape and opened the store. She'd done a great deal of thinking about herself, her mother, and her feelings for Ross. Talking to Dagna had helped. Her very wise grandmother had a way of slicing through the garbage and getting to the core of any situation.

Because business was slow for a Saturday, she had plenty of time for additional thinking. As she stocked the shelves and dusted books, she pondered her dilemma further, trying to be objective and brutally honest. The more she considered things, the more she decided that Dagna was right. She needed to follow her heart.

In trying to break the pattern of her mother's lifestyle, Susan was doing the very thing she sought to avoid—becoming an emotional cripple. Well, maybe cripple was too dramatic a term. She was becoming a turtle.

By late afternoon, Susan had decided that she was going to shed her shell and go for it. She was finished with running and hiding from life. By damn, she loved Ross. And while he wasn't safe like Thomas "Cold Grits" Rowe, he was nothing like any of the men her mother had married.

Ross Berringer was in a class by himself. He was thoughtful and fun and exciting. And despite his skirting the truth about the money, she knew he was honest. Deep down, she trusted him implicitly. He was a man of integrity and honor in the true spirit of the Texas Rangers. And, she smiled to herself, he was the sexiest man she'd ever encountered. He tended to be a tad overprotective, but they could work that out.

Yes, she decided, she would accept his proposal, but she would insist on several months engagement. Considering the short time they'd known each other, a long engagement made sense.

She closed the store an hour early and, feeling joyful, wheeled up to a corner flower market for a big bundle of flame colored gladioli. Tonight was going to be memorable. She was going to soak in a long bubble bath and dress in something guaranteed to knock Ross's socks off.

At the door of her town house, she tucked the day's mail under her arm and, humming and juggling the bundle of flowers, unlocked her front door. She'd just stepped inside and was about to close the door when a big silver Lincoln Town Car pulled into the parking space next to Ross's red truck.

When Ross, dressed in a well-tailored gray suit and a white Stetson, climbed out of the Lincoln, she was surprised. Susan had assumed he'd be slaving over their dinner by now. He'd intimated that he was preparing a special meal. When he opened the passenger door and a beautiful woman climbed out, she was curious. When the woman reached up and kissed him, she was stunned.

When the kiss turned into a full-fledged fervid embrace, she almost had a heart attack. The blood drained from her face, and the letters under her arm fluttered to the floor. Susan watched, horrified and heartsick, as Ross and the woman continued their passionate clinch. Finally they came up for air and started slowly up the walk to his town house, arms entwined around each other's waists and gazing into each other's eyes like long-time lovers.

Susan almost squeezed the stems off the flowers she held. Their scent turned cloying as her stomach churned and threatened to expel its contents. Her first impulse was to run as fast and as far from the humiliating sight as she could go. She clenched her teeth and fought the feeling.

As she watched Ross run his hand over the woman's hip, then bend and kiss her again, Susan's mortification changed to anger. Blazing, burning, consuming rage.

With blood in her eyes and her mouth set in a thin line, she stomped out of her entryway and strode toward the amorous couple.

"You snake!" she shrieked. "You low down philandering, good for nothing pond scum!" She whacked Ross with the fat bundle of gladioli, sending his hat flying. "Ross Berringer, I ought to shoot you with your own gun." She whacked him again.

"What the hell!" he roared, throwing his arms across his face as she beat him over the head.

"I can't believe I ever considered marrying

such a two-timing polecat! I can't believe I ever lost one minute's sleep over such a sorry specimen of manhood."

"Listen," he shouted, ducking blows, "you've got it all wrong. I can explain."

"You can't explain what I saw with my own eyes, you mangy aardvark." She whopped him about the shoulders, again and again until red flowers flew everywhere and the bundle in her hand was reduced to a few straggly stems.

The woman began to laugh, and Susan whirled on her. "There's nothing funny about this, you hussy!"

The woman laughed harder.

"Hoo-wee, what's all the commotion out here?" a deep voice behind Susan asked. "Sounds like a cat fight."

She turned and saw Ross standing in the doorway, a dish towel tucked into his belt. She looked at the Ross she'd attacked, then back at the one at the door. A terrible sinking feeling washed over her. "You have a . . . a twin?"

Ross grinned, then sauntered out to where the three stood. "Yep." He hooked his arm around Susan's neck and said, "Sin, this is my brother Holt and his new wife, Cory." He kissed her cheek. "This is Susan Sinclair, the love of my life."

Her gaze firmly anchored on the tips of her shoes, Susan tried a sickly smile but it never got off the ground. "Excuse me," she mumbled. "I have to go cut my throat." She twisted from Ross's grasp and bolted for the sanctity of her house.

With Ross yelling after her, she zipped by the camellia bush and through the door she'd left ajar. She slammed the door, locked it, and leaned against it, ignoring Ross's persistent pounding.

Maybe she could join the French Foreign Legion. Or become a missionary in Outer Mongolia. Or have plastic surgery and move to Rock Springs, Wyoming.

"Susan, dammit, let me in," Ross called.

"Go away, I'm sharpening a knife for hara-kiri."

"If you don't let me in, I'm going to break the door down. You know I'll do it."

He would, too, she thought. Sighing, she turned the lock and opened the door.

Ross stood there, dish towel still in his belt and hands on his hips. "You want to tell me what this is all about?"

"I just made an utter fool of myself. I thought Holt was you . . . and when he . . . when he . . . kissed her . . . I . . . oh, Ross," she wailed, stepping into his open arms, tears spilling down her cheeks. "You didn't tell me that you and your brother were identical twins."

He hugged her close and rocked her back and forth. "It's okay, darlin', it's okay."

"It's not okay. I'll never be able to face them again. I . . . I beat Holt over the head with a bundle of gladioli, and I . . . I called Cory"—her wails increased—"a hussy." She wept against his shirt.

He patted her back. "Now, now sweetheart. Cory understands. She didn't know Holt had a twin either, and the first time she saw me, she got madder than a wet hen and threatened to castrate me with an oyster shucker."

Susan drew back. "She did?"

He chuckled and nodded. "Get her to tell you about it. It was pretty funny."

"But I beat that bunch of flowers to a pulp over Holt. Do you think I hurt him?"

"Naw, babe. His head's as hard as mine. There's no harm done." He lifted her chin and kissed her. "You go dry those beautiful eyes and come on over to my place. I promise that neither of them is upset. I'll bet they're laughing about it right now."

"Are you sure?"

"Positive."

"You and Holt look exactly alike."

"Yep. We had a time playing tricks on people when we were kids. But there's an easy way to tell us apart. I wear a black hat, and I have a scar on my cheek." He touched the healing spot on his face. "And I," he added, kissing her, "am the one who loves you."

Late that night, long after dinner and shortly after Holt and Cory had gone, Susan and Ross sat cuddled together on his couch, sipping a glass of wine. He'd tossed his boots across the room, and his shirt was unbuttoned and pulled from the waistband of his slacks. Susan had kicked off her shoes as well and was rubbing her instep up and down his shin.

"I enjoyed myself this evening," she said.

"I'm glad." He kissed the tip of her nose.

"I like Holt and Cory. They didn't make me feel uncomfortable at all."

"They're nice folks." He kissed one eyelid, then the other. "And they have a very happy marriage."

"I could tell. I think Cory and I could be friends. Did you know she offered to blend a special perfume for me?"

"I like the way you smell now. Peach blossoms and spice." He nibbled her earlobe.

"You're a good cook."

"I'm not bad. I'd make some beautiful lady a fine husband." His tongue circled the rim of her ear.

She shivered with delight. "You know, I think this place would look better if you'd hang a few pictures." She stroked his bare chest and tangled her fingers in the dark silky hair that grew there.

He nipped the side of her neck. "Most of my stuff is still in Waco. I decided that since I've waited this long to have it moved, I could wait a little longer. I figured that if we're going to get married, we might want to buy a bigger house and combine our stuff. Or you might want to throw it all out and start over." His tongue made lovely circles in the hollow of her throat.

"Seems reasonable."

Ross went perfectly still. He pulled back and looked at her, his black eyes searching hers. "Does that mean what I think it means?"

Schooling her features into a guileless pose, she said, "I don't know. What do you think it means?"

"I hope it means that you just agreed to marry me."

A slow smile spread over her lips. "Since I love you like mad and want you to be the father of my children, I guess I'll have to."

Ross grinned from ear to ear, then threw back his head and let out a rebel yell that rattled the windows. "Hooo-wee! Hot damn!" He clutched her to him and hugged her so hard that she lost her breath. "Oh, darlin, I love you so much I'm about to bust. And I promise that I'll love you as much in forty years as I do now. More. I'll be the best damned husband to you that any woman ever had. Whatever you want is yours. All you have to do is ask."

His mouth moved over hers with a devouring hunger that sent heat racing through her like a brush fire. He stroked her with worshipful caresses and whispered love words in her ear until she was weak with wanting. Then he scooped her in his arms and stood.

"Where are we going?" she asked.

"To celebrate, my sweet Sin." He grinned, devilment lighting his eyes. "All night long."

# THE EDITOR'S CORNER

The coming month brings to mind lions and lambs—not only in terms of the weather but also in terms of our six delightful LOVESWEPTs. In these books you'll find fierce and feisty, warm and gentle characters who add up to a rich and exciting array of folks whose stories of falling in love are enthralling.

Let Joan Elliott Pickart enchant you with her special brand of **NIGHT MAGIC**, LOVESWEPT #534. Tony Murretti knows exactly what he wants when he hires Mercy Sloan to design the grounds of his new home, but he never expected what he gets—a spellbinding redhead who makes him lose control! Tony vowed long ago never to marry, but the wildfire Mercy sparks in his soul soon has him thinking of settling down forever. This book is too good to resist.

Fairy tales can come true, as Jordon Winters learns in award-winning Marcia Evanick's **GRETCHEN AND THE BIG BAD WOLF**, LOVESWEPT #535—but only after he's caught in a snowdrift and gets rescued by what looks like a snow angel in a horse-drawn sleigh. Gretchen Horst is a seductive fantasy made gloriously real . . . until he discovers she's the mayor of the quaint nearby town and is fiercely opposed to his company's plan to build new homes there. Rest assured that there's a happy ending to this delightful romance.

Terry Lawrence's **FOR LOVERS ONLY**, LOVESWEPT #536, will set your senses ablaze. Dave King certainly feels on fire the first time he kisses his sister-in-law Gwen Stickert, but she has always treated him like a friend. When they're called to mediate a family fight at a romantic mountain cottage, Dave decides it's time to raise the stakes—to flirt, tease, and tantalize Gwen until she pleads for his touch. You're sure to find this romance as breathlessly exciting as we do.

Janet Evanovich returns with another one of her highly original and very funny love stories, **NAUGHTY NEIGH-**

**BOR,** LOVESWEPT #537, for which she created the most unlikely couple for her hero and heroine. Pete Streeter is a handsome hellraiser in tight-fitting jeans while Louisa Brannigan is a congressman's aide who likes to play it safe. When these two get entangled in a search for a missing pig, the result is an unbeatable combination of hilarious escapades and steamy romance. Don't miss this fabulous story!

You'll need a box of tissues when you read Peggy Webb's emotionally powerful **TOUCHED BY ANGELS,** LOVESWEPT #538. Jake Townsend doesn't think he'll ever find happiness again—until the day he saves a little girl and she and her mother, Sarah Love, enter his life. Sarah makes him want to believe in second chances, but can her sweet spirit cleanse away the darkness that shadows his soul? Your heart will be touched by this story, which is sure to be a keeper. Bravo, Peggy!

Spice up your reading with **A TASTE OF TEMPTATION** by Lori Copeland, LOVESWEPT #539, and a hero who's Hollywood handsome with a playboy's reputation to match. Taylor McQuaid is the type that Annie Malone has learned only too well never to trust, but she's stuck with being his partner in cooking class. And she soon discovers he'll try anything—in and out of the kitchen—to convince her he's no unreliable hotshot but his own man. An absolutely terrific romance.

On sale this month from FANFARE are four fabulous novels. National bestseller **TEXAS! SAGE** by Sandra Brown is now available in the paperback edition. You won't want to miss this final book in the sizzling TEXAS! trilogy, in which Lucky and Chase's younger sister Sage meets her match in a lean, blue-eyed charmer. Immensely talented Rosanne Bittner creates an unforgettable heroine in **SONG OF THE WOLF.** Young, proud, and beautiful, Medicine Wolf possesses extraordinary healing powers and a unique sensitivity that leads her on an odyssey into a primeval world of wildness, mystery, and passion. A compelling novel by critically acclaimed Diana Silber, **LATE NIGHT DANCING** follows the lives of three friends—sophisticated Los Angeles women who are busy, successful, and on the fast track of romance and sex, because, like women everywhere, they hunger for a man to love. Finally, the ever-popular Virginia Lynn lets her imagination soar across the ocean to England in the historical romance **SUMMER'S KNIGHT.** Heiress Summer St. Clair is stranded penniless on the streets of London, but her terrifying ordeal soon turns to passionate adventure when she catches the glittering eyes of the daring Highland rogue Jamie Cameron.

Also on sale this month in the Doubleday hardcover edition (and in paperback from FANFARE in May) is **LADY HELLFIRE** by Suzanne Robinson, a lush, dramatic, and poignant historical romance. Alexis de Granville, Marquess of Richfield, is a cold-blooded rogue whose dark secrets have hardened his heart to love—until he melts at the fiery touch of Kate Grey's sensual embrace. Still, he believes himself tainted by his tragic—and possibly violent—past and resists her sweet temptation. Tormented by unfulfilled desires, Alexis and Kate must face a shadowy evil before they can surrender to the deepest pleasures of love. . . .

Happy reading!

With warmest wishes,

*Nita Taublib*

Nita Taublib
Associate Publisher/LOVESWEPT
Publishing Associate/FANFARE

**Don't miss these fabulous Bantam Fanfare titles on sale in FEBRUARY.**

## TEXAS! SAGE
*by Sandra Brown*

## SONG OF THE WOLF
*by Rosanne Bittner*

## LATE NIGHT DANCING
*by Diana Silber*

## SUMMER'S KNIGHT
*by Virginia Lynn*

**Ask for them by name.**

*New York Times Bestseller*
## TEXAS! SAGE
*by Sandra Brown*

Winner of every major romance writing award, Sandra Brown is an extraordinary talent whose wonderfully crafted love stories combine tender, unforgettable emotion with breathtaking sensuality. TEXAS! SAGE, the third book in her highly praised TEXAS! trilogy, features the "little" sister of the heroes of the first two books, Lucky and Chase, in a novel that is stormy, moving, and unforgettable.

In the following scene, set on Christmas Day, Sage has just received the worst present of her life—her fiancé, Travis, has just told her the wedding is off. . . .

Stepping away from a column, she wiped the tears off her face, refusing to indulge in them.

First on the agenda was finding a way out of this place. Hell would freeze over before she'd return to the party inside. Taking a deep breath of determination, she turned toward the corner of the veranda.

She took only one step before drawing up short.

He was loitering against the ivy-covered wall, partially hidden in the shadow thrown by a potted evergreen. There was, however, enough light spilling through the windows for Sage to see him well. Too well.

He was tall and lanky, even thinner than her brother Lucky. Although much of his hair was hidden beneath a damp, black felt cowboy hat pulled low over his brows, Sage could see that the hair above his ears was dark blond, shot through with streaks of pale ivory. Long exposure to the outdoors had left him with a deeply baked-on tan and sunbursts radiating from the outer corners of electric blue eyes, which were regarding her with unconcealed amusement.

He had a firm, square jaw that suggested he wasn't to be messed with, and a lean, wiry musculature that justified the arrogant tilt of his head and his insolent stance.

He was wearing a pale blue western shirt, with round, pearl snap buttons. His jeans had a ragged hem. The faded, stringy fringe curled over the instep of his scuffed boots, the toes of which were wet and muddy. His only concession to the chilly evening was a quilted black vest. It was spread open over his shirt because he had the thumbs of both hands hooked into the hip pockets of his jeans.

He was about six feet four inches of broad-shouldered, long-legged, slim-hipped Texan. Bad-boy Texan. Sage despised him on sight, particularly because he seemed on the verge of a burst of laughter at her expense. He didn't laugh, but what he said communicated the same thing.

"Ho-ho-ho. Merry Christmas"

In an attempt to hide her mortification, Sage angrily demanded, "Who the hell are you?"

"Santy Claus. I sent out my red suit to be dry cleaned."

She didn't find that at all amusing. "How long have you been standing there?"

"Long enough," he replied with a grin of the Cheshire cat variety.

"You were eavesdropping."

"Couldn't help it. It would have been rude to bust up such a tender scene."

Her spine stiffened and she gave him an intentionally conde-scending once-over. "Are you a guest?"

He finally released the laugh that had been threatening. "Are you serious?"

"Then are you part of that?" She indicated the sight-seeing traffic. "Did your car break down or something?"

While shaking his head no, he sized her up and down. "Is that guy queer or what?"

Sage wouldn't deign to retort.

The stranger smacked his lips, making a regretful sound. "The thing is, it'd be a damn shame if you ever got rid of those leather britches, the way they fit you and all."

"How dare—"

"And if you'd squirmed against me the way you were squirm-ing against him, I would have given you the sexiest kiss on record, and to hell with whoever might be looking."

No one, not even her most ardent admirers, had ever had the gall to speak to her like that. If she hadn't shot them herself, her brothers would have. Cheeks flaming, eyes flashing, she told him, "I'm calling the police."

"Now why would you want to go and do that, Miss Sage?" His usage of her name stopped her before she could take more than two steps toward the door. "That's right," he said, reading her mind. "I know your name."

"That's easily explainable," she said with more equanimity than she felt. "While rudely eavesdropping on a conversation that obviously went way over your head, you heard Travis call me by name."

"Oh, I understood everything that was said, all right. Y'all were speaking English. Mama's Boy dumped you, plain and simple. I thought I'd politely wait until he finished before delivering my message to you."

She glared at him with smoldering anger and keen suspicion. "You're here to see *me*?"

"Now you're catching on."

"What for?"

"I was sent to fetch you."

"To fetch me?"

"Fetch you home."

"To Milton Point?"

"That's home, isn't it?" he asked, flashing her a white smile. "Your brother sent me."

"Which one?"

"Lucky."

"Why?"

"Because your sister-in-law, Chase's wife, went into labor this afternoon."

Up to that point, she'd been playing along with him. She didn't believe a word he said, but she was curious to learn just how creative a criminal mind like his could get. To her surprise, he was privy to family insider information.

"She's in labor?"

"As of two o'clock this afternoon."

"She's not due until after the first of the year."

"The baby made other plans. Didn't want to miss Christmas, I guess. She might have had it by now, but she hadn't when I left."

Her wariness remained intact. "Why would Lucky send you after me? Why didn't he just call?"

"He tried. One of your roommates in Austin told him you'd already left for Houston with Loverboy." He nodded toward the windows behind which the guests were being ushered into the dining room.

"All things considered," he continued, "Lucky reckoned it would take me less time if I just scooted down here to pick you up." He pushed himself away from the wall, gave the dripping skies a disparaging glance and asked, "You ready?"

"I'm not going anywhere with you," she exclaimed, scornful of his assumption that she would. "I've been driving to and from Milton Point since I was eighteen. If I'm needed at home, my family will contact me and—"

"He said you'd probably be a pain in the butt about this." Muttering and shaking his head with aggravation, he fished into the breast pocket of his shirt and came up with a slip of paper. He handed it to her. "Lucky wrote that for me to give you in case you gave me any guff."

She unfolded the piece of paper and scanned the lines that had obviously been written in a hurry. She could barely read the handwriting, but then no one could read Lucky's handwriting. Lucky had identified the man as Tyler Drilling's new employee, Harlan Boyd.

"Mr. Boyd?"

One corner of his lips tilted up. "After all we've been through together, you can call me Harlan."

"I'm not going to call you anything," she snapped. His grin only deepened.

"Lucky offered me fifty bucks to come fetch you."

"Fifty dollars?" she exclaimed.

He tipped back his cowboy hat. "You sound surprised. Do you figure that's too much or too little?"

"All I know is that I'm not going anywhere with you. I'll drive myself to Milton Point."

"You can't, remember? You left your car in Austin and drove down here with Hot Lips." The lines around his eyes crinkled when he smiled. "I guess you could ask him to take you home. Although his mama would probably have a conniption fit if her little boy wasn't home at Christmastime. But you're not going to ask him, are you, Miss Sage?"

He knew the answer to that before he asked it, and she hated him for it. Throwing his body weight slightly off-center and relaxing one knee, he assumed a stance that was both arrogant and pugnacious. His thumbs found a resting place in his hip pockets once again. "Now, Miss Sage, are you coming peaceably, or are you going to make me work for my fifty dollars?"

She gnawed on her lip. He was correct on several points, chiefly that she was stranded at Travis Belcher's house. She wasn't about to throw herself upon Travis's mercy. Even though Harlan Boyd was a lowlife and her brothers had consigned her to spend time with him—something she intended to take up with them at her earliest possible opportunity—her pride wouldn't allow her to turn to a single soul in that house.

"I guess you don't leave me much choice, do you, Mr. Boyd?"

"I don't leave you any choice. Let's go."

She tried to go around him, but he sidestepped and blocked her path. Tilting back her head, she glared up at him. It was a long way up. She had inherited the Tyler height from her daddy, just like her brothers. There were few men she could really look up to. It was disquieting. So was the heat radiating from his eyes. So was his voice, which was soft, yet tinged with masculine roughness and grit.

"Given the chance you gave Loverboy, I'd've lapped you up like a tomcat with a bowl of fresh, sweet cream."

# SONG OF THE WOLF
## by Rosanne Bittner

They called her Medicine Wolf, and she was born at a time when buffalo herds stretched farther than the sharpest eye could see—a time when a people called the Cheyenne were a proud and free nation. Across the windswept plains, the white men were coming to seize the land and break a people's spirits—and their hearts. But fate would bring Medicine Wolf a love so deep and unyielding that nothing on earth could stop it . . . a passion she would traverse the land to find—and follow the haunting, heartbreaking path of the wolf to keep.

Medicine Wolf clung to her father's arm as he walked her to the edge of the village, where Bear Paw waited. Bear Paw would take her to the wedding tipi Medicine Wolf and her mother had erected out of sight of the village, along the river, a peaceful, pretty place, where they could be alone. It was nearly dark, and at last she would sleep the night in Bear Paw's arms! The thought brought a mixture of anticipation and apprehension. The splendid Bear Paw would be her husband!

They came closer, and Bear Paw stood next to the white stallion he had recently captured from a herd of wild horses. Medicine Wolf was sure he had never looked more handsome. He wore bleached buckskins, the leggings and fringed shirt beaded by his own proud mother, Little Bird. His long, black hair was tied at the side of his head, beads woven into it. A bone hairpipe necklace accented the muscles of his neck. Such a magnificent warrior he was! She wanted to shout and sing. Could any woman on earth be as happy as she was today?

She watched his eyes fill with pleasure as he looked upon her. Yes, today she was a woman. She wore a new white tunic her mother had made for her, for she had outgrown the one Old Grandmother had made so many years ago. Her wedding tunic was covered in circular designs of colorful beads, little bells tied into the long fringe at the sleeves and hem. Star Woman had worked on the dress for many months, in anticipation of her daughter's marriage.

Medicine Wolf's hair hung long and straight, a bright, beaded hairpiece tied into one side. On the belt of her dress she wore her little medicine bag containing the wolf paws, but she would not need their magic this night to keep her happy.

Black Buffalo stood beside Bear Paw. When Arrow Maker came close and held out his daughter's hand to her chosen husband, Black Buffalo chanted a prayer to *Maheo* to bless the marriage with much love and happiness. Bear Paw took Medicine Wolf's hand and could feel her trembling. He squeezed her hand more firmly, giving her a smile that told her never to fear him.

Black Buffalo finished, and Bear Paw captured Medicine Wolf's gaze as he spoke his vows.

"Forever I will love you," he told her. "I will provide for you and protect you. Your vision has been mine, and mine, yours. We have been one in heart and spirit for many years. Now we will be one in body."

The words made Medicine Wolf feel hot all over, and she struggled to find her own voice. "And forever I will love you," she responded. "I have loved you since I was but a child and you were part of my vision. I will keep your tipi warm and provide you with many sons who will one day become great warriors like their father."

"It is done," Black Buffalo told them. "Medicine Wolf now belongs to Bear Paw." He gave out a piercing cry, signaling the village.

Medicine Wolf and Bear Paw both smiled as those in the village whooped and shouted in return, expressing their joy. Black Buffalo and Arrow Maker left them. There would be much feasting and celebrating in the village this night, but the newly-weds would not be there. Already they could hear drumming, as Bear Paw took hold of Medicine Wolf and lifted her with ease onto the back of his horse. He mounted up behind her, putting strong arms around her and riding off into a thick grove of trees, toward the wedding tipi.

Finally, after all these years and all their dreams, they belonged to each other. They reached the secret place that belonged only to them, and Bear Paw lifted her down. Everything they needed was here, food, extra clothing, all was prepared. Bear Paw took his straw-filled saddle and the blanket from his horse and tied the animal to a tree. Medicine Wolf waited beside the tipi, her heart pounding, not sure just what he expected of her this first night. Would he understand her secret fears? White Horse's attack had left its stinging memory, had spoiled her vision of what this moment should be.

Bear Paw had said nothing all the way here. He had simply kept one strong arm about her waist, his lips caressing her hair. He came to her now, standing in front of her, drinking in her beauty with his eyes.

Medicine Wolf felt a sudden, overwhelming urge to cry. She struggled against it. What a terrible thing to do on her wedding night! She saw Bear Paw frown at the sight of her quivering lips and misting eyes.

He reached out and touched her face with a big hand. "So," he said, "you think I would just quickly take you for my own pleasure?" He pulled her close, crushing her against him. "I am not White Horse," he told her. "I have waited for this moment for too many years to let it be anything but perfect. No, my wife, I will not take you tonight. Tonight I will only hold you." He moved a hand to the shoulders of her tunic, untying the dress. "But I wish to look upon my beautiful wife."

She shivered, and silent tears of joy mixed with anger at herself for crying slid down her cheeks. He stepped back from her slightly, letting the dress fall. She heard him suck in his breath, but she could not bring herself to meet his eyes. Fire ripped through her when he touched a breast with the back of his hand.

"I am greatly honored," he said, his voice gruff with emotion. "Not only is my wife a sacred woman with great powers, but she is also the most beautiful Cheyenne woman who ever walked." He came closer and picked her up in his arms, carrying her inside the tipi.

A morning mist made the broad horizon beyond the river a gentle haze of green and gold, a soft, almost unreal scene. Medicine Wolf stood in front of her wedding tipi, where Bear Paw still slept. It still seemed incredible to her that he had kept his promise and had only held her last night. It was such a sweet, comforting feeling, and she knew she could always trust his word. But now she worried she might have disappointed him by not yet being fully a wife to him.

She walked farther away to pick up some wood for a fire. She should make Bear Paw something to eat. It seemed men were always hungry, or so it was with her father and brother. They would be camped here for one full week, remaining apart from the rest of the village, talking, getting to know each other. This was their special time. They would think only of happy things, and they would try very hard to make a baby. That was most important. She was anxious now for a child of her own, and nothing would make her prouder than to give Bear Paw a son. But that meant she must stop being afraid of mating. Last night her husband had shown her she could trust him. Now she would have to trust him to make a woman of her and not be afraid of the pain.

She turned to go back to the tipi when she saw him standing at the entrance, wearing only his breechcloth. His near-naked splendor almost took her breath away.

She moved closer to him and set down the wood, and she knew by the look in his eyes that he was a man wanting his woman. She told herself she would make him wait no longer. He walked close to her and took her hand. "We are friends, but still we are not lovers," he told her softly. "Last night I showed you I make no demands, for I honor you. But you are so beautiful, my wife, and I yearn to show you my love in every way."

Medicine Wolf wondered if she might faint. "It is not you that I fear," she answered, her voice sounding small and far away. "Nor do I fear becoming a woman. The only thing I fear is that I will not please you."

He put a hand to her chin, forcing her to look up at him. "I am your husband now. You can look me in the eyes, Medicine Wolf." She studied his handsome face as he spoke, the straight, white teeth, the true, dark eyes, the way his full lips moved as he spoke. "How could you think you might not please me," he asked her. "Never have I beheld such beauty. And our hearts have been as one since you were but a child. Last night we talked of many things. We know each other's dreams and visions, each other's desires, each other's hearts. All that is left is to know each other's bodies. And I promise you, Medicine Wolf, that in not too many days, perhaps only hours, you will want to share bodies as eagerly and as often as I. Do you think you are the only one who worries that you will not please? I, too, want to please you."

She smiled in surprise, her eyes moving over his magnificent frame. "How could you think . . ."

He put a finger to her lips. "Let me make love to you, my wife, before I die from the want of you. Last night was more painful for me than any injury I have ever suffered."

She swallowed, realizing it would be almost cruel to tell him no, nor did she want to. There seemed to be fire in his fingertips when he touched her shoulders then to untie her tunic. She let it fall away from her, and she wondered if he could hear her heart pounding, hoping that her legs would not grow so weak that she fell to the ground. She dropped her eyes again and felt his own eyes moving over her, drinking in her nakedness.

She was at his mercy now, but it was not like with White Horse. It was beautiful; gentle. He scooped her up in his strong arms as though she were a mere feather and carried her into the tipi, where he laid her on their bed of robes. She started to curl up, but he asked her to lie still. His eyes looked watery with a mixture of desire and near worship. "I have never seen such a beautiful creature," he told her, his own voice strained. He turned and dipped his hands into a wooden bowl of oil his mother had prepared for him, a mixture of water and fragrant oils from the stems of certain flowers. She had put it in a water bag for him, telling him it was good to use to relax his new wife and take away her fears. He had poured it into the bowl before coming for Medicine Wolf, determined that before the sun was fully risen, he would have laid his claim to her.

He turned back to her, touching her shoulders with his oiled hands. "Close your eyes and think only of good things," he told her. "Your muscles are tense, my wife, like mine get before going into a battle." He leaned closer, his hair loose now, shrouding her face as he touched his cheek to hers. "This is not a battle, my love. This is the most wonderful thing we will ever know."

# LATE NIGHT DANCING
## by Diana Silber

From the acclaimed author of *Confessions* comes a compelling novel of three friends, sophisticated Los Angeles women with busy, purposeful lives, who also live on the fast track of romance and sex—because, like lonely women everywhere, they hunger for a man to love.
The fast track can be dangerous. . . .

Cassie fights for sleep, but like a defeated, war-weary survivor she retreats, dragging back to wakefulness. Her eyes reluctantly open. She lies on her back staring up at continents on the ceiling designed by the sun in a gauzy shimmer through the thin curtains.

Seven-thirty! God! Who's mowing the lawn at seven-thirty in the morning?

A tall stranger in a Raiders T-shirt and well-worn jeans pushes the mower across her grass, winnowing neat rows. From the window Cassie charts the perfectly aligned patterns as she shouts down to the unknown titan, but the roar of the machine swallows her voice. Finally, cranking the window closed in disgust, she pulls on a robe and goes downstairs.

"Hey, who are you?" She has stormed out to the back porch and waved him to a stop.

After so much racket the quiet is stunning, and all of a sudden Cassie feels uncomfortable. She is crinkled from sleep, her short blond hair uncombed, her face without the least touch of makeup. She shifts her bare feet on the cool wood. "Who are you?" she repeats. "What happened to Yang?"

"I'm working for him now. The name's Jake."

Cassie tugs the robe tighter and folds her arms across her breasts. His blue eyes are flinty, chips of lazulite, and his gaze is unwavering. He doesn't look at her as Yang does, off to the side and unfocused.

"Do you have to start so early? You woke me up." The accusation, sleep-riddled, comes out too harshly. Foolishly she almost apologizes. The anger, grainy and directed at the mower as much as the man—can't they invent quiet machines?—begins to slip away from her. Faced with this Jake, she is somehow at fault. It must be the lost half hour of sleep. Every minute matters. Cassie loves sleep as a fat woman does ice cream. She envies insomniacs their endless nights of interrupted time.

She blames Mandy's going to college a month before for this weariness, but it had been the same when Doug left, three years ago last July. Whenever, in fact, life produces insoluble problems, sleep is the prescription. A stupid antidote; sleep is no solution at all, but an invisible weight will press her shoulders, bend her spine like a straw, as the air clots and she sinks down in her bed, grateful as a lover.

All this, she thinks, for a missed half hour!

Yang's Jake starts the mower again. She turns abruptly and leaves the cut grass blowing behind her.

By the time Cassie comes out again the gardener has gone. His truck no longer nudges its bumper to the curb. A collection of camellias in a tin can sits by the steps. Cassie almost trips over them. A penciled note sticks up between the leaves.

*Sorry.*

A nice gesture, Cassie thinks, carrying the can back into the house. She leaves it on the sink but brings the image of this Jake with her outside and down the steps. She sees the darkness of his eyes and the sweat shining on his upper lip and admonishes herself. Forget him! But he stubbornly clings in her memory.

Eve would tell her why. *Biology, pure and simple,* she hears Eve saying. But who was Eve to tell Cassie about biology? Cassie is the doctor; yet, *ha,* she hears Eve laugh in imaginary conversation, *you treat only women at the clinic and I'm the one who knows about men.* Did she? Did any woman?

Cassie hadn't known about Doug. Just as in magazine stories he came home every night for dinner. He never smelled of musky perfume. No long red or brown or any color but his own blond hair graced his jacket. He made love generously and on cue. Doug even brought her flowers when there was no occasion for gifts, except maybe to mark the stolen lunch hours shared with his lover.

But there weren't all that many roses, not enough for him to pack up and leave, saying, with the pretended grace of a man swept by poetry, *I'm in love with another woman.* Are there any words so brutal? Cassie would banish them, tries to with sleep, but they scar her in hard ridges and wait to greet her on awakening, the first bars of unharmonious dawn. If Cassie isn't careful, Doug's lips repeatedly form the impossible: *another woman.*

On principle she hates Tracy—Doug's lover and new wife— living in glassy sun-splashed splendor in Marina del Rey. Mandy, returning from twice-monthly visits, tells Cassie they aren't happy. Tracy drinks Diet Pepsi for breakfast and listens to Julio Iglesias. Tracy isn't neat. She ignores dishes in the sink and towels on the floor; she trails sand in from the beach. But Cassie recognizes Mandy's reports for the loving messages they are. Tracy is just a woman, *if another.*

Youngish and with a colt's awkwardness the one time she and Cassie met, Tracy is sullen. If she hadn't stolen Cassie's husband she would have captured someone else's. Tracy is a poacher. She displays the heavy-lidded drowsiness of a female too lazy to do her own legitimate hunting.

Cassie thinks too often of Doug. Not only in the first flush of shock and bereavement when, wounded, she stumbled, wept, invented heresies to believe in, but afterward. She recuperates because that is what women do when their men betray them; otherwise they are pitiful creatures, victims of those stubborn infections that won't respond to treatment. Cassie agrees with her well-wishers that Doug is a shit, better off forgotten, not worth a tear, a moment's unsound sleep. Not that her sleep is interrupted by Doug, by any marauder. Her sleep is medicinal. She should have given up the excess hours long since—oh, yes, she knows she is, in a manner of speaking, narcoleptic—and the dark dirges of unconsciousness. But she wants him back, not for himself but to eradicate the bludgeon of rejection, to be vindicated. A returning husband removes the stain of abandonment.

The Magdalene Clinic is south of National, a jigsaw-puzzle area of middle class and blue collar. A gynecologist-obstetrician, a woman's doctor, Cassie lives a life given to secrets. The words *breasts, uterus, cervix, ovaries, Fallopian tubes, vulva, vagina,* have everyday value for her, as do, among others, *dysmenorrhea, conception, pregnancy, abortion, hysterectomy.* There are so many diseases and conditions women endure that are foreign to men, so many malfunctions of their peculiar organs. The design of the female, though miraculous, is imperfect. She knows herself the pain of childbirth, PMS, the breathless waiting for the late stain on her panties. Faced with fluttering eyelids and sweaty hands, she explains the intricacies of birth control and wonders if the propagation of the species couldn't have been achieved in a more humane fashion. Why are women the bearers of the entire burden?

Despite Doug and the reality of her work, Cassie doesn't hate men. That would have been as foolish as loathing dogs because one bit her and others barked and leaped up with muddy paws. Men are only the opposite, the left to right, anodes to cathodes. They are just of a simpler construction.

All the physicians and nurses in the clinic are women, perhaps not deliberately—they know too much about sexual discrimination to practice it themselves, they promise one another—but they haven't sought out males either. There are Harry Bryan in administration and Chris Tomlan, the staff accountant, and some of the cleaning crew are male; but basically Magdalene is a woman's domain. Cassie spends her days in the world of females.

How do you think you'll ever find a man? Eve demands, brushing away Cassie's I'm-not-looking.

Eve, Cassie's best friend, is in real estate, a much more male-oriented field, as she puts it, which is lucky for someone married three times and constantly auditioning future husbands. Eve's hunger for mates border on the ridiculous, but she shrugs off Cassie's criticism by saying *Such is nature*. Men aren't necessary for every female at all times, Cassie counters in their running argument. She has had hers, plus marriage, a child. So what if there will be no long glide into twilight, days of gray hair and rocking chairs, the retirement porch of shuffling memories. She is certainly better off than her other close friend Nona, six months shy of forty and panicking, her biological clock ticking as loudly as a timer on dynamite.

The phone rings as Cassie buttons her white coat. It is Eve to remind her of dinner at seven. "You're driving. Okay? But tell me, before I hang up—met any good men?"

"Since I talked to you yesterday?"

"Well, miracles are known to occur. You could have bumped fenders with Sylvester Stallone. He's single, at least momentarily."

She has no time for Eve's teasing. "I have patients waiting."

"And I have a house weeping to be sold."

Men. She is getting as bad as Eve, catching herself as she goes through the day wondering whom she might meet. What is this, a sea change, a strange scent on the wind? Like Mandy, is she tricking herself into forgetting?

# SUMMER'S KNIGHT
## by Virginia Lynn

A New Orleans heiress, Summer St. Clair never dreamed that fleeing from an arranged marriage would leave her stranded, penniless and alone, in the unfamiliar streets of London. But her terrifying ordeal soon turned into breathtaking adventure when she captured the glittering eyes of an untamed rogue. In the following excerpt, Summer finds an unexpected savior in a shabby inn. . . .

"Are you, by any chance, on your way to London, sir?"

He wasn't. He'd intended to avoid the city completely; but now, looking at this wide-eyed girl with the slightly tilted eyes and winsome smile, he hesitated in saying so.

He sat and watched the girl for a moment. He toyed with the idea of seduction. She looked luscious. Her hair was an odd color when dry, with thick strands of varying shades of gold alternating with darker tints of brown, as if she had been in the sun a great deal. But her complexion proved that she could not have lingered in the sun; it was pale and creamy, without a single blemish, except perhaps, for one or two freckles dusting the end of her straight little nose. She had high cheekbones and a full, sultry mouth; her eyes were wide, thick-lashed, unusually blue, a deep color that made him think of summer bluebells.

Jamie sighed. She was beautiful. Really beautiful.

"Yes," he heard himself say, "I am traveling in that direction. Why?"

"Would it be possible for me to travel along with you?"

It was impossible to refuse. He smiled. "Of course."

Summer hesitated, then added in a soft, urgent voice, "I'm in something of a hurry, sir."

"Are you?" His dark gaze riveted on her mouth, and he wondered if her lips tasted as luscious as they looked. "Why are you in a hurry, lass?"

Jamie's gaze snapped back to her eyes when she said, "I must meet a ship before it sails."

"A ship?" His brow lowered slightly. "What ship?"

"The *Sea Dancer*. You see, I came over from America on her, and if I can just reach London before she sails again, I will be able to return home."

Her words were fast, running into one another so that he had a little difficulty in following them, but somehow, it was what she *didn't* say that interested him most.

Leaning forward, he clasped his hands on the top of the table. "How will you buy passage if you have no money?"

Summer hesitated a shade too long before saying, "The captain is a . . . friend."

"Ah. A *friend*." He thought he understood. Of course she would have a protector. Any female who traveled with an unreliable maid and a small cloth bag holding only a few items of clothing could not be as well-bred as he'd first thought. A pity. Or was it? If she was not some convent-bred miss from a fine family, it certainly left the door open to seduction.

Summer recognized from his expression what he thought and opened her mouth to explain. Then she shut it again. Why not let him think that she had a lover? It might save her from what she saw in his eyes if he thought she was already spoken for.

She met his gaze steadily. "I'm not exactly naive, sir. I know what I'm about in life, if you understand."

That single black brow rose, and he nodded silently, seeming to digest this bit of information as she had wished him to do.

"Do you have enough money to pay the coach fare for both of us? I have a necklace that we could sell, perhaps, if you don't. . . ."

Startled by her assumption of his inability to pay, he started to correct her, then paused. It had been a few years since he'd had to live off his wits; it might amuse him to do so for a while now. Especially since it would put him in the position of gallant cavalier to a young lady in distress. It wouldn't hurt the seduction he planned at all. In fact, he found he liked the idea quite well.

"Don't barter your necklace yet," he said. "I think I have enough to pay our way."

"Good. When we reach London, I will see to it that you are repaid for your kindness," Summer said earnestly, and saw an amused light flare in her benefactor's eyes.

"Will you, lass?"

She seemed surprised. "Of course."

A smile flickered at the corners of his mouth, and his voice was deliberately husky. "I won't charge highly for my services, lass. Just a simple kiss will be payment enough."

"A simple kiss?" Summer echoed, sensing that with this man who fairly radiated male vitality and virility, there would be no such thing. She bludgeoned her quickening pulse into submission before saying coolly, "I find your suggestion vulgar and shocking, sir!"

"Come, lass—it will be such a small thing to do for a man willing to put himself out to escort you safely to London, don't you think?"

Summer thought it over for several moments, then knew she had little choice. "Very well," she said with the air of a martyr, "I accept your terms. One kiss, and no more, and you will take me to the port of London."

"You may not want to stop at a single kiss," he said. "Have you thought of that?"

"Not at all." She glared at him for a moment, then gave a soft sigh. "I'm ready," she said, and leaned across the table. She closed her eyes and put up her face for his kiss, tensing against it. In spite of herself, her pursed lips tingled with anticipation as she waited for him to kiss her.

Jamie stared at her. "I've no intention of kissing you here in the middle of the common room with the innkeeper and half his staff watching us. I'll collect my payment when I'm ready."

Summer's eyes snapped open, and she felt very foolish. Her high cheekbones reddened, and her mobile lips tightened into a line. She'd not thought of that. But perhaps he had the better idea, especially when she noted the faintly malicious, watchful eyes peering at them from across the room.

She nodded stiffly, and the quick glance she gave him was eloquent. "Agreed, sir."

Jamie watched her with veiled eyes, knowing what must be going through her mind. She was right. He did want her. His body ached with the wanting; he shifted uncomfortably. It should be a fair enough trade. She wanted to go to London; he wanted to bury himself inside her.

She rose from the chair, then, struck by a thought, she looked at him. "By the by—what is your name?"

His dark brow quirked in amusement. "Ah, so you've grown curious about me, have you? James Douglas Cameron, at your service," he said with a sweeping bow. "And I love a challenge, lass. It makes victory all the sweeter."

# FANFARE

## Now On Sale
### *New York Times* Bestseller
# TEXAS! SAGE

☐ (29500-4) $4.99/5.99 in Canada
### by Sandra Brown

*The third and final book in Sandra Brown's beloved TEXAS! trilogy.
Sage Tyler always thought she wanted a predictable, safe man . . . until a
lean, blue-eyed drifter takes her breath, and then her heart away.*

# SONG OF THE WOLF

☐ (29014-2) $4.99/5.99 in Canada
### by Rosanne Bittner

*Young, proud, and beautiful, Medicine Wolf possesses extraordinary
healing powers and a unique sensitivity that leads her on an unforgettable
odyssey into a primeval world of wildness, mystery, and passion.*

# LATE NIGHT DANCING

☐ (29557-8) $5.99/6.99 in Canada
### by Diana Silber

*A compelling novel of three friends -- sophisticated Los Angeles women with
busy, purposeful lives, who also live on the fast track of romance and sex,
because, like lonely women everywhere, they hunger for a man to love.*

# SUMMER'S KNIGHT

☐ (29549-7) $4.50/5.50 in Canada
### by Virginia Lynn

*Heiress Summer St. Clair is stranded penniless on the streets of London,
but her terrifying ordeal soon turns to adventure when she captures the
glittering eyes of the daring Highland rogue, Jamie Cameron.*

# FANFARE

**FANFARE**

## Sandra Brown

_____ 28951-9 TEXAS! LUCKY ..................... $4.50/5.50 in Canada
_____ 28990-X TEXAS! CHASE ..................... $4.99/5.99 in Canada

## Amanda Quick

_____ 28932-2 SCANDAL ............................. $4.95/5.95 in Canada
_____ 28354-5 SEDUCTION ......................... $4.99/5.99 in Canada
_____ 28594-7 SURRENDER ........................ $4.50/5.50 in Canada

## Nora Roberts

_____ 27283-7 BRAZEN VIRTUE ................ $4.50/5.50 in Canada
_____ 29078-9 GENUINE LIES ..................... $4.99/5.99 in Canada
_____ 26461-3 HOT ICE ............................... $4.99/5.99 in Canada
_____ 28578-5 PUBLIC SECRETS ............... $4.95/5.95 in Canada
_____ 26574-1 SACRED SINS ...................... $4.99/5.99 in Canada
_____ 27859-2 SWEET REVENGE ............... $4.99/5.99 in Canada

## Iris Johansen

_____ 28855-5 THE WIND DANCER ......... $4.95/5.95 in Canada
_____ 29032-0 STORM WINDS ................... $4.99/5.99 in Canada
_____ 29244-7 REAP THE WIND ................ $4.99/5.99 in Canada

**Ask for these titles at your bookstore or use this page to order.**

Please send me the books I have checked above. I am enclosing $ _____ (please add $2.50 to cover postage and handling). Send check or money order, no cash or C. O. D.'s please.

Mr./ Ms. _____

Address _____

City/ State/ Zip _____

Send order to: Bantam Books, Dept. FN, 414 East Golf Road, Des Plaines, IL 60016
Please allow four to six weeks for delivery.

Prices and availablity subject to change without notice. FN 16 - 12/91

# FANFARE

**Ask for these titles at your bookstore or use this page to order.**

### Rosanne Bittner

_____ 28599-8 EMBERS OF THE HEART . $4.50/5.50 in Canada
_____ 29033-9 IN THE SHADOW OF THE MOUNTAINS
$5.50/6.99 in Canada
_____ 28319-7 MONTANA WOMAN ........ $4.50/5.50 in Canada

### Dianne Edouard and Sandra Ware

_____ 28929-2 MORTAL SINS ..................... $4.99/5.99 in Canada

### Tami Hoag

_____ 29053-3 MAGIC ................................... $3.99/4.99 in Canada

### Kay Hooper

_____ 29256-0 THE MATCHMAKER, ......... $4.50/5.50 in Canada
_____ 28953-5 STAR-CROSSED LOVERS .. $4.50/5.50 in Canada

### Virginia Lynn

_____ 29257-9 CUTTER'S WOMAN, ........... $4.50/4.50 in Canada
_____ 28622-6 RIVER'S DREAM, ................. $3.95/4.95 in Canada

### Beverly Byrne

_____ 28815-6 A LASTING FIRE ................. $4.99/ 5.99 in Canada
_____ 28468-1 THE MORGAN WOMEN .. $4.95/ 5.95 in Canada

### Patricia Potter

_____ 29069-X RAINBOW ............................ $4.99/ 5.99 in Canada

### Deborah Smith

_____ 28759-1 THE BELOVED WOMAN ..$4.50/ 5.50 in Canada
_____ 29092-4 FOLLOW THE SUN ............. $4.99/ 5.99 in Canada
_____ 29107-6 MIRACLE .............................. $4.50/ 5.50 in Canada